POKEWEED

AN ILLUSTRATED NOVELLA

BRIAN L. TUCKER

ILLUSTRATIONS BY KATERINA DOTNEBOYA

Black Rose Writing | Texas

The final approval for this literary material is granted by the author.

First printing

This is a work of fiction. Names, characters, businesses, places, events and incidents
are either the products of the author's imagination or used in a fictitious manner.
Any resemblance to actual persons, living or dead, or actual events is purely
coincidental.

ISBN: 978-1-68433-109-3
PUBLISHED BY BLACK ROSE WRITING
www.blackrosewriting.com

Printed in the United States of America
Suggested Retail Price (SRP) $14.95

Pokeweed is printed in Chaparral Pro

Praise for **Pokeweed** -

"*Pokeweed* is a fascinating account told by Ezekiel "Z" Snopes, who must choose between revenge and forgiveness, in this wonderfully illustrated novel about the French-Eversole feud from the 1880s in Eastern Kentucky." – Sybil Baker, author of *While You Were Gone* and *Immigration Essays*

"I hope this one sells a million copies." – Donald Ray Polluck, best-selling author of *The Devil All the Time* and *The Heavenly Table*

"The western world of *Pokeweed* is a refreshing burst of energy to the young adult world! The characters are charming, and I was ready to jump right in with my own shotgun to end that war! What a great read for my first western novel." – Hannah Rials, author of Young Adult *Ascension* Series

"Brian has my permission to write." – Chris Offutt, best-selling author of *Country Dark*, writer for HBO's *True Blood* and *Weeds*

"Brian L. Tucker is writing about Eastern Kentucky in original and interesting ways, and *Pokewee*d is a perfect example of that. I'm excited about this newest book and eager for what Tucker does next. You should be, too." - Sheldon Lee Compton, author of *The Same Terrible Storm*

Praise for **Swimming the Echo**

"*Swimming the Echo* had me hooked from start to finish! The story kept me intrigued about what would happen next and the character development was outstanding. It's the first book I've read by Brian Tucker and after reading this one I bought another one of his books. Highly recommend." – Eric Overby, author of *Journey: Poems*

Praise for **WHEELMAN**

"Brian has a bouncing [debut] book!" – Robert Olen Butler, Pulitzer-Prize winning author of *A Good Scent from a Strange Mountain*

"Tucker spins a meaningful yarn about a dude struggling to create and maintain an identity in the face of serious danger and overwhelming loss." – Sevan Paris, author of *Superheroes in Prose: Series*

To Dad, who knows not all Westerns happened West of the Mississippi.

The Dark and Bloody Ground, so the teacher romantically said,
But one look out the window, and woods and ruined cornfields we saw; A
careless-flung corner of country, no hope and no history here.
– Robert Penn Warren, *American Portrait: Old Style*

...Kentuckians sustain themselves principally by hunting and fishing. They
are remarkably good shots and effective assassins.
– New York Times (November 20th, 1878)

All the rest of the way I travelled alone with God and the mountains.
– Dr. E.O. Guerrant travelling from Jackson to Hazard (August 1892)

*Friends, one and all, I want to talk to you a little before I die. My last words on
earth to you are to take warning from my fate. Bad whiskey and bad women have
brought me where I am. I hope you ladies will take no umbrage at this, for I have
told you the God's truth. To you, little children, who were the first to be blessed
by Jesus, I will give this warning: Don't drink whiskey and don't do as I have
done. I want everybody in this vast crowd who does not wish to do the things that
I have done, and to put themselves in the place I now occupy, to hold their hands.*
– Bad Tom Smith (June 28th, 1895)

"Pokeweed is a native American, and what a lusty, royal plant it is!"
– John Burroughs, *A Year in the Fields*

POKEWEED

CHAPTER ONE

My name is Z Snopes, and my sister was killed for a measly five Greenbacks.

It happened in Kentucky. A place the Iroquois called Ken-tah-ten. Ma told me and sis once it had to do with tomorrows. I found out later a Cherokee called it *a dark, bloody ground*. I think that one sums it up best.

CHAPTER TWO

Sissy was young. She had her whole life ahead of her. We was just passing through Hazard to home, when it happened. Her pony, Squeak, spooked and tried to toss her and me. Which was rare. I grabbed Squeak's bridal and snapped her reins down to calm her. But the gun blast had already sounded.

I still flinch every time I hear a revolver. Sissy flew backwards before I knew what'd hit. Squeak took off into the branches and brambles along the path. My ears rang. My nostrils cringed at the gunpowder smell. I'd fallen from the pony and ran back to Sissy lying in the fallen leaves.

CHAPTER THREE

Sissy *was* Isabel Snopes. She died on September 28th, 1888. I felt the warmth of her final breaths as I leaned in, with her in my quivering, blood-stained arms. She mouthed something I couldn't quite make out. I wanted to ask her again, but she gave up the ghost. I cried on top of her chest wound, because what else could I do? She met the Lord a few seconds later. She was twelve years old.

I don't remember any other gunshots. The villainous bastards just shot that one time like they wanted to save bullets, and I tended to my sister in the haze of smoke. I couldn't hear any voices, but I knew they were there still. Must've raided my saddlebags while I helped Sissy into the Promised Land.

CHAPTER FOUR

How do I know it was five Greenbacks?

Well, it's all we had between us. I know Squeak wasn't carrying anything else, because Sissy asked me to pack light. Just the essentials. Beef jerky, a canteen of tepid water, some oats for our mount, and a money note. That's it. They killed her. No questions asked. Then. I guess they left. Because they weren't there when I wiped my eyes and scooped my Sissy from the wet leaves.

Pop and Ma were torn up about it, but it was a tough time already. Sissy's departure from this earth was one less mouth to feed. We were eight before. Now, just seven. We buried her in the backyard near the Sumner Place – miles of wooded coverage and timber. Sissy would've liked it, because she always did whilst alive.

Her favorite verse was always the one about God watching over the sparrows and talkin' about not worrying, because God looked out for his own. *Yeah, I think, real good job of that the other day.* But, I went to Sissy's grave and tried to remember her laugh. Even though she was small, barely a hundred pounds, she had the best laugh. If you got her tickled like I did with a joke, it sounded like *Ee-ooo*, almost like a soft hiccup. It made me laugh, too.

But, as I'd tried to keep the cooling blood from running out of her, I thought of a different verse. The one about an eye for an eye and tooth for tooth. I thought about the sounds of gunfire. Pop's Colt revolver resting above the fireplace on the mantle. *She was worth more than the sparrows.*

CHAPTER FIVE

After Sissy Izzy's burial, life went back to normal. Or, my family tried to will it that way. We went to church. We stabled Squeak indefinitely like a tainted pony, spooky to look at. Preacher Dooley preached on bloodlust, against revenge. His beady, grey eyes hovered toward me and bore into my hairless chest. I held his steely gaze as he went on preaching every Sunday.

While I slept at night, I still heard Dooley barking Proverbs. He spat about man's ways versus God's. How we don't ever know exactly what's right and we don't get to be judge, jury, and executioner. But, I laughed and said, "Tell that to Sissy, Dooley," and Dale, my oldest brother, shook me awake saying, "Stop carryin' on, Z!"

If I could dig up Sissy and ask her what she'd said, before the end, I would. Like Jesus leaving the tomb and telling everyone it was okay. But, I couldn't bring myself to get the shovel. Pop would whip me six ways to Sunday. I wanted to tell him I was thirteen, nearly a man, but his mind was elsewhere.

Squeak stamped her foot and shook her head at my approach. She's *growing* wilder already, I thought.

"Sissy'd smack you silly for trying to bite me," I said out loud.

The barn was empty except for us. Squeak ate a sugar cube I brought. I leaned in and smelled her hickory smell like Sissy used to.

"Good, Squeak. My Squeak," I tacked on in my best Sissy tone, before my voice croaked.

CHAPTER SIX

It's hard to go back to farming after you lose someone. Dale pushed me to keep up with him, as we set tobacco. All I thought about was that Colt revolver, sweating stinging my eyeballs. Pop scolded Dale for not scolding me enough. I started missing spots to set the plants. Then, I set them too deeply. Pop yelled and halted progress. He took off his belt, and I knew what came next.

We didn't have time to dillydally, and I knew that. We had to put food on the table. The blessing (and curse) of being one of eight, now seven. We were unpaid, hired hands all part of the Snopes family homestead. Only Sissy got to rest now, and that thought gave me a good hope. My backside was sore from the lashings Pop gave, but I was more focused. The tobacco had to be set before dark.

The tobacco grew, and one night I saw it from the kitchen window. I thought how Sissy wouldn't grow past her slight frame. The grass was now deep green, with flowers blooming on the hillside where her body rested forever. God helped her grow above ground after all. The goldenrods were yellow and almost the same color as her favorite sunrises. Almost. There was pokeweed sprinkled here and there, too.

I spotted the Colt in a flicker from the fireplace. It hadn't moved in a long while. Pop let cobwebs ensnare it. I rose up from the cool, dirt-packed floor of our cabin and reached for the mantel.

"What're you doin', Ezekiel?!" he snapped.

That's my full name like the prophet in Bible times. Sissy first called me Z, and everyone else followed suit.

I imagined the heft of the pistol.

Mose—my youngest brother, along with Dale's help—tackled me to the dirty ground.

Pop stepped over my torso and laid a good smack on me, busting my lip open. "You ain't listenin' with them ears the good Lord gave you! Wastin' crops is one thing. Disobeyin' me is something else. I'll take you out behind the smokehouse and learn ye. You want that?"

I squirmed a little, but my brothers' eyes spoke volumes. Dale looked at Pop, instead of facing me. And Mose fought back a tear and cleared his throat.

If Mose could summon the strength, his voice would say, "I miss her, too, Z. Not just you."

Pop spoke, his lips moved, and I didn't respond. I didn't even wipe my bloody lip. I just waited for him to tire out. Eventually he did, and Dale's grip slackened, and I rolled over and heard Pop spin the gun's cylinder and release the shells to his pocket and snap the revolver closed. When I finally looked, the cobwebs were broken, the gun gone.

My lips crusted over and hurt when I tried to yawn the next morning. My finger touched the dried blood, and it felt hard right in the middle of my bottom lip like a divot. My tongue raked across it and the taste was salty iron. No one else stirred, and the wood smoke was finally petering out inside the living room. The smoke, which normally cheered me on Saturdays, made me sad.

CHAPTER SEVEN

People in our holler talked about the Civil War still. Many said it would never go away even though it was twenty something years past. Things couldn't keep going the way they were, they said. When I listened enough to care, I heard someone say Yanks were like Brits. I was too divided in my own soul to care. Sissy was more important to me. Not some grudge.

I replayed that fateful trail ride over and over in my mind's eye. Ma told me to get my mind back on stripping tobacco before frost came, before Pop whipped me again. Sissy was gone, she said. My heart longed for her laugh, and the tobacco growing up to shoulder height made me sick.

"Work harder, boy, if you want supper," Pop scolded.

The tobacco made its way to the barn loft. Dale took on the role of overseer and tried to make Pop's job easier. He liked to pretend *he* would whip me.

"Lay off him, Dale!" Mose defended, but he wasn't a match. He gave up fifty pounds to our big brother. Real lashings found me still, but my soul couldn't muster the same work ethic. I was broken inside.

Sissy's grave was no longer yellow with goldenrods. The cool weather, and the first frost, withered and coaxed the plants to sleep. I visited her on a Tuesday before Thanksgiving. She was six feet below but felt a million miles. The Sumner Place grew quiet, and I was glad winter came next. I knew I should assume caretaker next spring. Sissy deserved that much—a clean burial plot.

"What was it you said that day, Sissy? Before you...?"

I avoided chores and sat out behind the smokehouse. Hoping Pop would bring the belt and show me something akin to pain. His stripes reminded me of living. But, he didn't come. He fed the cows hay in the barn and Dale slopped the hogs. I could hear the animal calls and the sounds of buckets being emptied. Mary and Holly waved to me on the woodpile and Laverne snickered, accusing me of not doing chores. Said I was in big *t-r-o-u-b-l-e*. I told her to git. I was busy being hid.

I scrunched the frosty ground underfoot and watched the first flakes of December fall. Pop reminded me that our fall harvest could've been better had I daydreamed less. *Work for the Lord*, he said.

But who was working for Sissy?

They shot her off Squeak. Dead. It could've been me. Should've been. In a way, it was. I felt dead. But, I wasn't covered in a burial mound. There's just snow on top my shoulders now, my wavy brown hair. The wood smoke smell brought back too much hurt. Sissy wasn't in the cabin laying logs on the hearth.

There were so many questions I wanted to ask God. And I did ask in my sleep. Things like:

Why's Pop so evil?

Will we ever get away from this damned tobacco?
Who was that man who shot Sissy?

Usually the answers didn't come straightaway, but I prayed all the same. Dale would hit me when I snored, but I got right back to dreaming either way. God listened. So I spilt and he listened. And I woke up and sometimes remembered what I jawed on about the night prior. Sometimes all night. That morning I remembered. Because I saw his picture on the front of the Hazard paper.

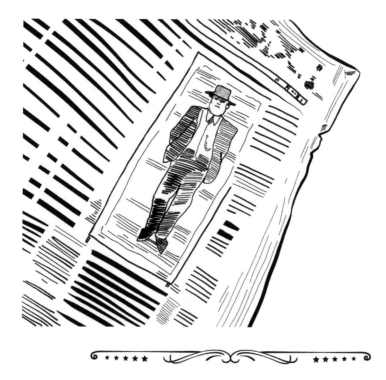

Oz Munford, the paper read. He was wanted for murders in the counties to our east, including Breathitt.

I didn't see him that day Sissy was shot. I didn't even hear him. But I knew. Like how a person just knows. As if God was saying *That's the man!* And my dream connected to that paper in Pop's hand like the snap of fingers. It was Oz. He was one of 'em.

When everyone was full and away from the table, I eyed the folded paper and scooped up the front page and took in Oz's ugly mug, his scraggly whiskered chin. The picture made him even more villainous like a demon. I vowed those five Greenbacks would come back to haunt him and his.

"That's Pop's paper," Laverne tattled, loud enough to be heard in the living room. I shushed her and swatted at her backside. She ran to Ma with a loud wail. I didn't care. I was suddenly ambitious.

There was justice in taking Squeak out of her stall with my folks shouting loudly behind me. I said, "Giddyup!" and the pony responded with a short, sideways buck. Her wildness almost got me tossed, but I held on and steered Squeak down our road and away from the Sumner Place. I waved to everyone but especially to Sissy's grave.

CHAPTER EIGHT

Some of the families in Kentucky hollers really had trouble with one another. The nation was something far away, in D.C. Recovering from the war still, they said. *Our war never stopped*, I thought. Names like French, Eversole, and Bad Tom Smith were more front and center in Hazard. People in the hills took notice. I tried to be a good student and listened to the names being called. No one named Munford. Not yet.

The Peacemaker was tucked against my belt, weighing on my breeches. Reloaded, and with a box of bullets as well. I kept thinking about the sparrows, and Sissy always laughing at my jokes. I didn't feel bad about my theft. It felt like a just cause. One Ma should've supported.

I was hungry and hadn't thought about food. Jerky or corn pone would've been welcomed, but I forgot it in my hasty exit. Sissy's ghost wouldn't let me rest. Oz Munford was out there. I pushed the pain down and gulped a lukewarm mouthful of saliva. I whipped Squeak and rode into Hazard by nightfall.

I'd never fired the gun before. It would prolly kick like a mule. Pop always said it did. Dale said he'd shot a few rounds along the fencerow. I remembered Mose nodding in agreement. Brownnosing no doubt. I'd find out how it kicked when I fired it *myself*. The gun clanked and clawed at my hipbone and I stopped at the saloon. Squeak watered up at the trough and I figured I'd brush her down later.

I felt out of place the moment the doors swung to behind me. Dale told me of promiscuous ladies who sold things on the top floor of the saloon. Mr. Johnson was the barkeep, and he kept business going by proferring drinks nonstop. I stuck out my chest, tipped my cowboy hat back from my eyes, and walked brazenly to Johnson.

"Don't serve young'uns," he answered, waving a hand.

"I don't want one, Mr. Johnson," I said, lowering my voice, trying to make it growl, hiding my tremble. "Just a little information about someone...a wanted man you might've seen."

Those playing cards closest to the bar paused in their hands. One gentleman looked from Mr. Johnson to me to see what would transpire.

"Get out. Don't meddle."

I encouraged him there wasn't a meddling bone in my body. I flashed the .45 beneath my waistband. The man at the table tossed his cards and slowly started to rise. He had a badge, and I guessed he was Hazard's newest sheriff.

Mr. Johnson held up his hand, waved his head. "I can talk to him outside. No trouble, Phil."

And the lawman slowly sat, and ever so reluctantly, went back to his cards. I followed Mr. Johnson to the hitching post, and Squeak, outside the saloon.

Mr. Johnson asked if I wanted to die. *Was I trying to?* I shook my head and pointed my index finger at the pony.

"See her?"

Mr. Johnson stared me down, silent.

"Her name's Squeak," I said. "She's my sister's ... or was."

"What you want little man?"

"I want Oz Munford."

Mr. Johnson stared at the pony and back to me. He lit a cheroot cigarillo and took a mighty long draw. Then, he shook the match out before it burned his finger. The rich, hickory smoke curled out past us into Hazard's sky. "You know his dealings, then?"

"Firsthand...more than I'd like to," I swallowed.

Squeak looked up expectant for a treat. We avoided her glance and she went back to the water.

"You only have the one piece?"

"'S all I need, Mr. Johnson."

"Think you're tough, huh?"

I didn't answer. Just watched his smoke rise.

"You know what those boys'd do to you, if you got too close...started throwing accusations?"

I asked for a smoke, and he said get lost.

I started undoing Squeak's rope, when Mr. Johnson gripped my wrist too tightly.

His harsh, tobacco breath said, "Munford, ain't worth it, kid. Believe me."

I begged to differ. Oz Munford and his crew shot Sissy from point blank range without a word of warning. Just leveled her out with the earth. I didn't get my goodbye. And, I didn't expect much. But some things a person had to pay for. This one named Oz. He had to pay.

I scolded Squeak for drinking so much. A pony could founder like nothing else, and she drank half her body weight in water while we'd stopped. I heard her stomach sloshing, as I turned her away from the hitching post. It made me mad. Plus, Mr. Johnson's words still stung. I kicked her harder than I should've. She bucked and I heard another voice call out.

"What you whipping that pony for?"

I turned and it was Phil. No longer playing poker but leaning on the swinging saloon doors. "She doesn't know why you're being such a lout. Stop it."

"You ain't Pop, and I wouldn't listen if you was," I said, turning red in the face.

"Don't matter. You got no right to be cruel to that animal."

I held back on the reins and knew he was right. Squeak frothed at the mouth, and her insides shook with water. "Whoa. Whoa," I soothed, patting her belly. "I'm sorry. Whoa, girl." Eventually she straightened out, and Phil came over to my stirrup, taking Squeak by the reins.

"Well?"

"Well. I hear you're looking for trouble."

"Not trouble. Just a man. Him and any other who wants to see me."

"Think you're the law, boy?"

"I got to be tough." And I did. Every bit of my soul knew it. It was sink or swim every day.

"And you want Oz Munford?" Phil said, dropping his voice to barely a whisper.

"You have good ears."

"I'm law in Hazard, now," he said, patting Squeak's mane. "I keep peace."

"I figured that," I agreed. "Not wanting to do anything wayward. I guess you know about Sissy Snopes?" I added, looking him fully in the eyes, pushing my cowboy hat back again. "How Oz and company did it?"

Phil tipped his hat. "Surely."

"Then, I reckon we're settled on what needs to be done?" I told more than asked.

"Let justice work itself out. We're watching those boys mighty close here in Hazard and out past Perry County and beyond. We know they're getting tangled up in all kinds of mischief, and I've heard tell they're trying to cheat farmers of coal land, too. B. Fulton French is behind it all. I'm gonna catch him and everyone riding with him."

I looked at this new sheriff. *Who was he kidding? Didn't he know who his neighbors were?* I laughed and caught myself. If it wasn't so sad, and I hadn't lost so much already, it might've been funny. But it wasn't. I said, "Let go of the reins, *Phil*," snapping Squeak away from the lawman's soft, unworked hands.

CHAPTER NINE

The saloon had failed me. I was no closer to the man I sought, and I couldn't get the image of Sissy, on this pony instead of me, out of my mind. Every time I kicked Squeak, said 'Let's go!' I thought of how she did it different, better. Her innocent laugh. I dismounted and re-hitched the pony to a different post farther down Main Street.

Hungry and restless I went on foot to the edge of Hazard and climbed the steps of the Good Counsel Church. Usually I'd avoid bringing violence to the Lord's house, but I was fresh out of options, and I needed someone holier than myself to guide this mission. Before I could even push the big, oaken door, the inside screeched open and a hand waved at me.

"Come in. Come in. Keep the cold air out, lad."

I stepped into the empty sanctuary and noticed all the ornate woodwork on the pews, the pulpit, the Lord's Supper table.

"Figured I'd meet you where you were," the gentleman continued. "Saw you climbing the steps, and you looked plumb frozen. Take a seat. We'll talk," he waved to the front pew.

I sat and removed my hat. Jesus was on the cross above us – the front of the room, best seat in the house.

I made him wait. Not because I'm mean by nature, but I didn't really know how to go about asking what I really wanted. Blood. Retribution. Justice served. The communion table etched with *Do this in remembrance of me* served as a warning against the work I undertook. The man sat and waited and looked at Jesus above us. Not rushed at all, it seemed.

"Do you know the Snopes?" I finally said.

The preacher folded his hands in front of his legs and turned to face me. "Snopes...Reg and Linda Snopes? Of course I do. Good, good people. Salt of the earth," he added, keeping his gaze on me. "Do you?" he asked in return, and I couldn't tell if he was bluffing.

"I'm a Snopes," I said, like a confession almost. "Z Snopes...Ezekiel, I mean. I guess you heard about—"

"My heavens yes. Y'all have been on the prayer list here since that fateful day."

I didn't even try to play dumb. I folded my hands together in front of me. Jesus had blood on his forehead where the thorns crushed his eyebrows. A mockery like Sissy was, I felt. My blood boiled, as I looked at the crucifix. "What's the Bible *really* say about getting even? Like is it..."

He stood up and went to the pulpit, where I imagined a Bible was already open, waiting to be digested.

Not a sermon, I thought. But part of me wanted one. One like Preacher Dooley never offered. A genuine one with real conviction. Something to take my mind away.

He cleared his throat, and he picked up the largest text I'd ever seen. I didn't know Bibles could grow that big, but this one was. Every bit of fifteen pounds and he sat down beside me again, with his finger on a verse.

It was from Ezekiel like my name. He started to explain the verse when the heavy doors pounded open.

The preacher stood and looked to the uninvited. Snow flurries chased the new arrivals into the sanctuary and littered the floor with wet, cold precipitation.

A trio of rough looking misfits let the heat escape out the church doors, unconcerned with weather. I wanted to defend God's space, but the man in front caught my eye. He was scruffy, his chin possessing hairs sprouting out in every direction. His eyes were grey and squinty. *Oz.* I tugged on the preacher's shirt and wanted to share this, but he waved me off.

"Gentlemen, can I help you? Please. Step inside and let's keep the heat with us," he added, trying to usher them in. "We can take our time and sort this whole business out."

Those words caused Oz to spin to the man. "I've already sorted it out, preacher. This young'un wants to duel. 'S what I hear tell. Right?" he said, looking to me in the front pew.

I swallowed and gave my best steely gaze. When I found my voice I said, "Who gave you that news, Munford?"

"I have eyes and ears around Hazard, sonny. Mr. Johnson for one. Heck, even law listens when we tell 'em to," he laughed.

His constituents joined in and made their voices heard throughout the Lord's house.

The eerie sound sickened me, and I felt for my Colt. It was sweating against my waistband. I felt the moisture on the pistol grip. The preacher saw my hand and shook his head curtly.

"I'd listen to preacher man, Z," Oz encouraged, his voice like a snake, drawing out the sound in a hiss.

"Let's just you and me settle this outside," I said, hiding my shaking hands behind my back. "No one else needs to die, because of you."

"No one else will," he said, matter-of-factly. "Well besides..."

"Then, let's go," I pointed for the door.

He waved me ahead, and we went out into the frigid clime. His men stayed in the church with the preacher.

"Should of killed you both that day in the woods," Oz said, over the wind. "I guess this is what I get for saving a bullet, huh?"

I wanted to fill him with lead, but I wasn't sure if I was quick enough. I didn't know if he'd want to quick draw, but I knew he was a gunman, being tied to a gang and all.

"You can use your lead today, then, can't you?" I coaxed, trying to sound tougher than I was. I noted the two revolvers on his hips and pushed away the image of him fanning them, mowing me down like Swiss cheese.

"Lil fool," he sneered. "You ready to meet your Maker? Here at the church steps an' everything?" he grinned behind crooked teeth.

Before I even saw his tight-lipped smile falter, I had the heavy Colt out of my waistband, hammer cocked, and trigger smashing down on lead. *Blam. Blam. Blaaam.*

He fell, and I almost rejoiced too soon, because I saw a flash from the corner of my eye, and I heard voices shouting, "Get him. Don't let the twit get away!"

I heard another report as a white, searing pain sliced my side. The rest of Oz' group was taking bead on me, and one bullet grazed my ribcage. I needed cover. My only option was the church, but they blocked it, standing on the steps. Blindly I fired the rest of my shells at them, over my shoulder.

I could've sworn I heard the preacher cheering, but I've been known to lose my bearings once in a while. My shots didn't connect, because they returned volleys of their own. I looked for the box of shells in my pocket. Reloaded the last three, and I could hear Sissy telling me "Good job, Z. Now git your hide to cover!"

I held my ribcage and loped down Main Street. Checked the coast on both sides of the alleyway and saw Squeak stamping restlessly. "Well, let's go, girl," I whispered. I unwrapped her reins from the post and jumped on.

"Giddyup, hoss!" I screeched and created my own dust trail out of Hazard. I didn't know all of the damage, but I knew I'd just gunned down Oz Munford with a Peacemaker.

CHAPTER TEN

The bonesaw, Doc Branson, worked all hours. I'd remembered Pop talking about getting sewed up there after a drunken brawl or two. I tried to recollect where he was situated on the hillside, but there was just one light burning at this hour. I dismounted and pecked on the door. An elderly, brittle-boned man answered and held an almost melted candle to my face.

"Yeauh? Another skirmish over booze? Won't let an old man rest will ye?"

I didn't answer, just followed him inside.

My side didn't hurt too much. My pride wasn't even hurt, because I'd seen my foe perish. But, I figured this was as good a place as any to hole up.

Seeing as how I got away with no more than a limp, and they, the other creeps, wouldn't suspect I'd be dumb enough to stay out in the open like this. But, I was. *Who were they gonna look to for leadership now anyways? Oz was dust.* Then, I remembered who Phil said they were all riding with – the treacherous snake, B. Fulton French.

Bonesaw Branson was from Bransons as far back as the land first settled, called Kentucky. A Branson lived in every holler. He asked to see the injury. I reluctantly moved my hand over my ribcage, and he yanked shirt fabric from congealed blood and I whooped and yelped.

I must've passed out, because when I came to Bonesaw wasn't around, and I had bandages and a deep, red circle where more blood leaked into new gauze. *Oz got me better than I thought.* When I looked over at the table, I saw my hat and Colt. I wondered if more bullets could be had from Bonesaw, but I thought better of it. It might be disingenuous to ask the healer for artillery. More wounds he might not mend later.

"I don't want trouble," a voice said, as I reached for the gun. I looked in the direction of the voice. Bonesaw was pointing at my Colt piece. "I hear tell from a few folks earlier that a whippersnapper is on a vendetta. Looking to make even agin' a bad bunch...any truth to that?"

I'd normally defend myself. If it was me against Dale and the others at home, I'd open my mouth with venom, but I knew Bonesaw wanted peace, wanted to go back to bed. I could see it in his tired eyes, his receding hairline. Like his body knew it should be at rest, even if Hazard wouldn't let him.

"Make peace with God and go home, son. I don't want a shootout in my cabin."

I wanted to tell him I didn't want another either. The one was enough. I didn't have it out for any more brigands – just Oz. But, I saw my fault. My error in judgment. Trouble came in pairs like the loading of animals into Noah's wooden ark. Not one but two critters for each scuffle. Sissy dead. Oz dead. The math of sins. Fult French would find out.

"Besides, that lil pony of yourn done ran away. Somethin' must've spooked her. You'll be on foot now," he said, without expression.

"Shit," I heard my voice croak in the still air. "Where?"

Bonesaw stared at me but didn't say. Just shook his head.

The one remaining piece of Sissy gone. My hat *thumped* down on my head. Bonesaw bent over to look at my brown eyes. Least they were brown the last time I'd checked a mirror. It'd been a long while. Sissy told me I had chocolate pudding for eyes.

"He won't quit as long as he knows you draw breath, boy. You know it, don't you?"

I reckoned I did. Told him with a grunt and shuffled to collect my coat, now sporting a gaping hole. The wooden planks felt good on my calloused feet. He whipped the December air to life – flinging the cabin door open. I bid him a better morning and thanked him with a tip of my hat.

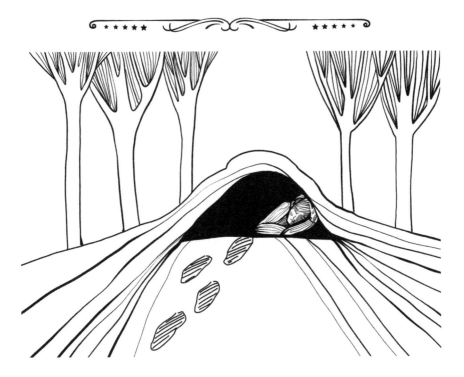

The small cave jutted out just enough to be seen from my vantage. I had subtle fears my brothers had imparted of troglodytes ravaging me in my sleep. But, I was too tired to care. I was an outlaw. At least in the eyes of Phil and Hazard courts. I'd just shot a man in cold blood and fled the scene.

It wasn't cave dwellers who kept me awake but winter itself. That cold, grizzly old man huffed at me and blew flakes of frigid ice into my cave and kept me up and pacing in the wee hours like an angry bear destined to wander the earth seeking hibernation.

My stomach roared, and I accidentally tore at the bandage and made it bleed anew. Then, like the winter storm, my hunger abated and numbness went away. *Maybe frostbite?* But, I didn't care. I was glad for the reprieve. I felt like a somnambulant doomed to sleepwalk forever.

I don't recollect climbing (or falling) down Shady Mountain, but I ended up at the mouth just the same. The sun peeked through the thin, wispy stratus clouds and cast what little daylight the mountains allotted. I felt a tingle in my hands and knew it wasn't good.

A house with smoke billowing out its chimney loomed large and wondrous, and without a glance inside, I barged through the front door, knocking the lock, latch and all, onto the warm floor.

I heard a gasp, and my head knocked against the planks of the home's floor, and I slept the deep sleep of one fully concussed.

When I came to, my clothes were on a chair, and I shifted in the soft featherbed. The quills gently poked me through the ticking. I looked underneath and saw I had all my digits and limbs still. Ole man winter would have to try harder to kill me.

A pair of olive eyes spied me from the bedroom's corner, and a voice scolded the eyes saying, "Maggie don't stare. Get him some water!"

Olive eyes left, and my heart tried to follow her out the door. The word became flesh and it was a lady Ma's age, and I saw it was Ms. Layton – teacher of Hazard's one room schoolhouse. I quit going, but I remember her telling a story or two when I did go. Always favored her voice. It was soothing, even when it scolded.

"Maggie's my daughter," Ms. Layton answered. "Wants to become a midwife. You're a good subject, Ezekiel Snopes. Comin' in half frozen like you did."

I wanted to say something brave. Talk about why I was risking my life, but she didn't pay no mind. She asked why I shot Oz Munford. Didn't I know all of eastern Kentucky was after me.

I very much doubted that but cringed all the same. Pulled up the warm covers and waited for her to leave.

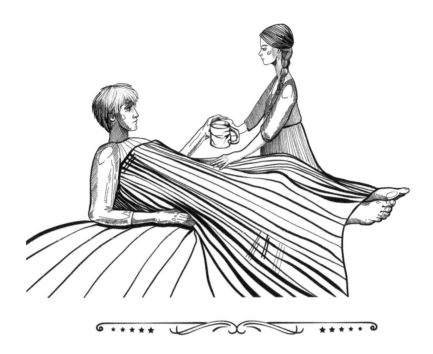

Olive eyes returned, introduced herself, and ran her hand across the quilt. It unnerved me more than the gunfight had, and I wrestled the covers away.

"I'm Z Snopes. You might not want to get too close."

"Momma told me who you were. I remember you from the schoolhouse. We're about the same in age."

"I'm in trouble," I said, puffing out my chest. "The law wants me now."

"Momma said that, too. Said we can't keep you hidden out. It's un-Christian going agin' the law. Did you do those awful things they said?"

Her eyes sized me up, becoming narrower, and I hated to see the green hue hide itself.

"What're they saying?"

Before she could answer, I added, "I'm sure a bunch has been made up. I'm not in the wrong, *Maggie*." Saying her name made me feel better, jolted me like stealing a cup of Pop's morning coffee.

"You have to go, before the sun rises full. Momma told me to tell you there's jam and biscuits in a basket for you. You best eat before people come."

"I'll be fine," I tried to tell her, but I didn't feel that way. Going home would only bring on Phil and the law. Surely Pop and Ma knew of my actions. But, it would make it worse if I went back and hid among them.

No. I figured it was only decent that I accept Ms. Layton's gift, her daughter's heeding, too, and head out for cover in the hills again. Her eyes gave me motivation. *Would she go with me?* I shook my head knowing the notion was silly. Half-cocked.

I couldn't ask such a thing anyways. *And why would she even consider?* I was a wanted gunman now.

CHAPTER ELEVEN

The Layton's saw me out. I felt December around my ankles, where my socks had plenty of holes. The chill made me want to run back inside. Throw another log on their fire. But, I saw the olive orbs and knew Maggie deserved better. I needed to be a man. Own up to my plight. I was on a collision course with some of the meanest folks to visit these woods. If lawman Phil wouldn't stand in their way, or couldn't, I would. I just wished I wasn't alone.

The truth of the matter was:

I'm not sure how I bested Oz
How I got away
Why I was still alive
Why Branson, and the Laytons, took care of me
Where I should go next

Before shooing me away, Ms. Layton stepped out onto her frozen porch and shut the door behind her. Maggie was inside peering out. Ms. Layton looked me in the eye and said, "Troxell's might have some supplies for you. Now go."

Of course. The hubbub of shooting and killing Oz drove me senseless. Troxell's was the only trading post left in Hazard—the spot for more bullets.

Troxell's was stocked, but I forgot I had no money to my name. Sissy's money was long gone. And I couldn't part with my piece. I couldn't downgrade to a .22. I *needed* the Colt for what I was up against. Fult French wouldn't make concessions.

Troxell saw me eyeing the ammunition. He, along with everyone else in the town, must've known I was wanted by more than one party. He saw me fumbling for change that wasn't there. He knew the look of a beggar. Before I could even mumble an excuse, I picked up two boxes of shells and he looked the other way. I scavenged the boxes quicker than I meant to—looking desperate as a mare in heat.

As I set the boxes into Ms. Layton's loaner basket with the biscuits and such, Troxell's hand held onto it. He finally made eye contact and said, "You have my prayers, Z." Said it like I was a man about to be hung for crimes I didn't feel wrong in committing. I grunted and stowed the bullets away. I made for the door and tipped my, too big, hat.

What a world where lead, steel, and gun smoke were common and almost friends. Like they connected us to the afterlife so directly that I couldn't even walk down the street without feeling for my six-shooter, touching the handle like I might shake hands with a dear friend. My dueling partner. *If I'm fast, and it's accurate, we'll win the day. If the cold weather causes the gun to resist and my hands to grope, we lose.* It was a team effort just to survive in Hazard.

The aperture in my ribcage stung. I bit my lip and swore I'd calm down after this business was over. Maybe go visit Maggie again.

It seemed like fate was going to encourage me to use every bullet I'd been given by Troxell. *I needed a plan.* Because, just then I saw two men approaching me in the alley and they were the same ones who ran with Oz that day I shot him dead.

The creeps approached, one raised a hand like we were friendly. I think more so, because they didn't recognize me at first. Didn't think I'd be dumb enough to show myself on the Hazard streets so soon after our skirmish. The hand raiser dropped his wave slowly, as he saw my face. Quickly he lurched for his holster and fired at me, knocking over a barrel instead. I fell behind the barrel and fumbled in the street for my spilled shells.

Bullets whizzed by in a continuous volley, and I waited for one to travel through the barrel and lodge into my thigh, or worse, my noggin. But, they kept traveling past, or into deep grooves of the barrel's wood, sending splinters up with every shot. When I remembered the shells still in the revolver's chamber, I waited for a ceasefire and lurched up and pulled two shots at the hand raiser and one at his friend. Hand raiser dropped like a flour sack, and the second man suffered a leg shot. He screamed and hollered for mercy. I stuffed what fallen shells and biscuits I could back inside the pack and made for the edge of town. Now, I figured I was definitely in trouble.

Another verse came to me after Sissy fell that day. It was the one where Esau hated Jacob to the point of wanting him dead. I don't know why that one wouldn't let go. It wasn't like I hated my brothers. I loved Ma and my sisters. Sissy the most. I didn't feel like some blessing had missed me really. Or, maybe I did. Maybe I felt *just* that way. Like God watching the sparrows and Sissy still dying, maybe I reckoned I missed the good life.

CHAPTER TWELVE

Pop worked like a mule every day on our farm. Dale, too. Even our kinfolk would pitch in when they visited, because they knew how tough Snopes had to work just to have a little. And we barely did that each year. We were a long line of sharecroppers.

The problem with hate was it'd eat a person up. It ate Pop up. I saw it eating Dale before I left home. Mose would be next, if'n he didn't leave. Boys harden up like criminals. I didn't want to be a criminal. I wanted to shoot Oz, and I did. Now, I wanted to be left alone.

I missed Squeak. Her smell. The saddlebags to put the bullets in. Just the company. I tried not to not think of Maggie, and the cold helped me a lot. I stuffed my hands into my breeches to keep warm, but it chilled me deeper. I thought about how much it'd take to get someplace warm. Maybe a hot bath in Washington, D.C. Join Mr. Grover Cleveland at the capital. Talk about the nation.

If I told the President bout my Sissy shot dead, would he approve of my actions? I wanted someone else's word to weigh in. I prayed God would speak. My hands and feet were numb. My backside was frozen to the pointy grass blades on the hillside. Moving around would just draw attention. That's how I shot Oz's friends. My mind was focused on the wrong things. I forced the warm, wood-burning stove out and pondered the pain of Pop's black leather belt. That helped.

My guess was it'd take the second man a bit to convalesce and warn Fult French's outfit. He would show them the bullet hole in his leg. *What if they went after Ma and the rest?* It wasn't too far-fetched. French's gang might hurt 'em.

That tore into me even worse. I hated Pop most days, but I respected the hell out of the rest. Even Laverne and her big mouth. I needed to keep them safe. I had to – *for Sissy*. It was a pledge I made aloud, my breath blowing icicles almost the moment the hot air left me. Somehow, I would.

But how does someone stop evil? All I could keep my mind on was hating like Esau did. I wanted to stomp the face of everyone attached to Sissy's death. I vowed to myself that I'd take out all of Appalachia if I needed to. Winter and the cold couldn't stop me. I shivered from a gust of wind. It made its way inside my patched, tattered, and re-patched wool coat. The sweat froze my wavy hair to my forehead.

My legs stove up like my hair and refused to move along the ridgeline. I fought 'em inch by inch and considered rolling down the snowy bank like I'd done as a child.

How cold could I get? How much below zero before I lost a toe, or worse? I didn't need all my toes, I guessed. God gave room for a few mishaps here and there. An accident with a glass jar. A mistake in the field with the plow. A person could still balance themselves without some of the middle ones. I'd seen a friend lose a toe, when a Clydesdale stepped on it. He said the big toe and pinkie were the two most important, because they were on the ends. I didn't put a lot of stock in what he said. But then again, I still had all ten.

Keeping my legs ambulatory made the going easier. The blood pumped and churned like an engine I'd heard Pop talk about once. The *chug chug chug* he got all worked up about at the dinner table. He saw an engine once at a shop in Hyden. I pumped my legs and made myself go around the ridge and grappled with the pine trees for leverage.

The biscuits I devoured in no time. The jam, too. And, I found two leather pieces and took them out of the basket and saw them for what they were. The Laytons were a godsend. *Gloves!* Ma told me we had angels walking amongst us, and I suddenly believed her. I thought of Maggie sneaking the pair to me, and I warmed even more.

My covered hands brought life back into my extremities. I rubbed the rawhide scent over my face and my patchy, blonde stubble. I wished there were a half dozen more biscuits to scarf down, but the crumbs in the basket were all that remained.

The calvary didn't come into the woods at all. Neither did the devil. It was just me and the birds that hadn't flown south. I saw a bobcat, but she didn't pay me no mind. I used to have nightmares of bobcats feasting on me for some reason. They pulled at me and gnawed on my hide. I didn't imagine I tasted too good, but their eyes lit up and finished me off every time, before I awoke.

Mose wanted to be just like me. Dale thought I was nuts when I'd told him about my imagined duels with the cats. I hated that Mose was left to fend for himself around Dale and Pop. I wanted to protect him. Maybe Ma would take him under her wing. Teach him how to sew and love him more than Pop. But, I knew it wouldn't ever come to that. I was his lone protector. So, it hit me like a ton of bricks.

My best bet was to grope around the Sumner Place—our home, the woods behind Sissy's burial plot—waiting for French's gang to come at us as a family. He would look there next, if I stopped showing myself in Hazard. I'd survived a few days on the frozen hillside. It was the only thing I could figure. I had to risk my family again to make it all go away.

CHAPTER THIRTEEN

I poked my head out from the woodpile, behind the smokehouse. A fresh snow had kicked up three inches since night, and I knelt on the boards, the snow melting into my pant leg.

Raucous laughs met my stiff ears. Laverne and the girls were chasing Ma around the kitchen. I saw Pop stomp through the room after them with his belt. I recalled the scent of oil husked across my back, leaving welts. Twas how he kept the belt limber, he said. I wanted to storm inside and tear into him, but I had to hold back. I needed to take everyone by surprise. *That's how it'd work best*, I told myself.

Even the gloves froze onto me, and I heard the groans of the girls, as Pop lay into them with the belt. Ma yelled for him to quit and he lashed her as well. *God, please.* But the *whacks* continued for minutes. Long minutes. Then, at the exact moment the snow stilled the screams abated. I didn't trust my hearing so I peered out again to glimpse the house. The cabin was placid like Kentucky Lake where we one time went and tried to learn how to swim. Dale almost drowned and tried to take me with him. It wasn't a good memory.

Pop had tired out.

He was drinking water from the metal ladle on the back porch. Dunk after dunk he gulped and guzzled. This was as good a time as any for me to take him. I had the pistol. But, I breathed in deep. Took my frozen digits away from the gun. I scanned the front of the house and imagined Ma soothing the girls. Mose getting the bandages together for her. Dale watched Pop from the kitchen. Wondering how he could make his ole man proud. *Could he ever? Could any of us? No.* He just hadn't learned that lesson like I had.

If Fult French & crew knew how much brokenness we had already, they might not even darken our doorstep. But they would. All the same. A grudge burns in a murderous heart until it's removed by an outlaw, or, it's gotten its revenge.

Pop didn't have other guns in the house. I was their only hope, and they didn't even know it. Kneeling on my frozen board waiting for all hell to break loose, I wished I had a clock. Some way to tally up how many meals I'd missed. It didn't matter. Sissy was worth more than anything I'd ever eat. I would die for her. I whispered in the silent, December air, "I *will* die for you," and my voice sounded funny, too loud. Dangerous even.

Good, I thought. *Dangerous is good. Dangerous will keep you alive.*

That word gave me chills. Apart from the cold. It was that single word: *alive*. Running from Pop and him running from the war and Rebels running from Yanks and families running from French and him running from God. It was all of us trying to stay alive. We thought money or time could make us alive. God could if we found him. They all hid like a fox most days. Now, I felt it fully and deep in my bones. Down where the marrow was inside the skeleton. I remember Mama sucking the marrow from a turkey leg and letting it season a gravy. She said, "That's where the strength is...in that marrow." That's where I wanted to be—alive in the marrow.

If winter didn't kill a body, someone like B. Fulton French would. I felt the need to kill any and all like him. If I survived this winter, I'd go after whatever else the devil drew a bead on me with. I had my Colt and my gloves. I had a hunger that wasn't going away anytime soon. I was desperate enough to do anything.

Then, I saw her.

Laverne that pipsqueak. Looking at me through the kitchen window. She waved, and I knew Ma was gonna know. Laverne couldn't keep her big trap shut for nothing. She never had. Why should she this once? She looked at me and waved again. Instead of ushering her with just a wave, I waved and put a finger to my chapped lips.

"Shhh," I said to the house. "Shhhh. For the love of God in heaven, Laverne, Shhhh."

She mimicked me and ran off into the house like a thunderclap, as if Pop hadn't just unleashed war a few minutes before. "If you want to stay alive, Vernie, you'll keep yourself quiet. This one time, big mouth," I prayed as much as I threatened her beneath my breath. I was no good to her dead. Dead was dead to us all.

She either hushed or was ignored, because Pop didn't arrive. I sat on the woodpile and waited and waited and nothing stirred inside the Snopes cabin. I was grateful for this small mercy. *Laverne, you snot-nosed brat, I don't know if I should thank you or not.*

The weather didn't care for me one bit. It huffed and puffed and slammed against my threadbare wool coat. It gave me a jolt with every new surge of air, every gust of malice. If the weather had a personality, and I believed it did, it was Ebenezer Scrooge from a story Ms. Layton once read aloud. Stingy and harsh in all the wrong ways at Christmastime.

I don't recollect all the details, but I do remember Scrooge's greed. His visit with three ghosts. A trinity of reminders. He was meant to relive all his worst moments. He was never happy. He made many people hunger and thirst. Thinking of this made my mouth water, as my mind locked in on a big Christmas feast—the one with Tiny Tim. My stomach slammed against by back, and I grabbed at my midsection.

Laverne didn't join me. Pop wasn't wrestling me from the woodpile either. Each hunger pain jabbed at me like a rod twisting my insides around. I didn't believe I could take much more. I wanted some form of an answer.

And I got it.

In the most unexpected way, too. A cardinal flashed across the all-white sky. Bright and red and singing for his mate. It caught me off guard, but I recognized it wasn't a mate's call but a shriller warning instead. There was someone disrupting the frightened bird's path. No. Several someones. An unwelcome party was upon me.

Horses' snorts preceded their stamping feet, their shifting saddles and squeaks of leather. It was a convoy of men I didn't recognize, but it didn't matter. I knew what they wanted and who sent them.

No one in my family needed to be harmed. I was their target. I was tired of fearing for more spilled blood.

I retrieved the revolver and made sure it was full. *Snap.* I stuck a complete reload in my coat pocket. I made sure there weren't any holes in my coat. Then, to be safe I filled the other pocket with a third volley. The remainder of shells I left on the lumber pile. *If need be, I'll come back. If I'm not already gone.*

A horse whinnied—releasing its hot breath. Two others snorted to match. I hunkered down and checked my peripheral against what I saw to be five men approaching. *Five!* I was the only gunman, and my family was defenseless. *Why would French do it?* But, I knew the answer already. He didn't care one bit.

Another glimpse at the party, and I didn't see a *true* leader. No one, like who I imagined French to be, at the front of this pack. He was too busy swindling landowners out of coal rights somewhere else. This was of little concern to him. Simple math.

It emboldened me even more, and I thought to already pull the Colt's hammer back. As I did, I heard someone shout, "Z Snopes! C'mon out, and we can spare yer folks. Leave the rest of 'em alone. Honest to God we will."

The voice hollowed out along the ridgeline, and the only remaining image was the puffs of smoke from our home's fire.

They know you're in there, Pop. Don't be a coward. Say something before you get lit up!

But, I knew better than anyone how he'd react. He'd play possum instead of fessing up.

The candles went out in the living room and the kitchen. Only the smoky wisps remained. *Coward even when death comes knocking,* I thought. *Say something to ward them off.* But, he didn't. And a rifle fired from one of the horsebacks and connected with the cabin's wooden exterior. A chorus of shrill cries erupted inside and Dale stormed out alone.

"Is this him?" one rider asked.

The self-appointed leader shrugged, mumbled something to his group. Then turned to the approaching Dale and held out his hands. "Whoa, there. This don't have to get ugly. We have word to collect Z Snopes and be on our way. Are you him?" the man asked, spitting a mess of brown liquid from his mouth to the snow.

Dale shook his head. "I ain't, but I can help you. I know where he went. And, if you promise to leave, I'll give you word for word what he said to me the other day. Deal?"

I knew Dale was bluffing, but I was mute at my spot. He was on his own in this lie.

The ringleader waited for more.

Speak you moron, I wanted to lash at Dale. But, he just gawked at their guns. Then, his fingers went to his pockets and the man said, "Ah ahh," and shook his head. He didn't know Dale didn't have a piece on him.

"Spill it, kid."

Dale's lip quivered, and I knew he was gonna lie. He was a terrible liar. It was the face he always made before laying down a sorry poker hand. *He was as good as dead.*

I knew I needed to act fast, before he wedged himself in too deep.

I barely heard, "He...um, Z, is...see, he went to Hazard like a few days ago sayin' he was done with us and—"

"Out with it, kid. Don't lie or we'll put some souvenirs betwixt your sorry eyes!"

I heard the gun click—hammer cocked back, tight. This was it. The whole world.

I looked to the edge of the house and calculated my steps. A distance I'd memorized while playing hide-and-seek a thousand times with cheating brothers. Fifteen steps. I could draw, shoot, and lunge fifteen paces before any return fire would have time to get me. I already knew I needed to draw down on the leader first. Disorient the whole enterprise. So, as Dale ho-hummed about my whereabouts, I lined up as pretty a shot as my numb wrist would allow my ungloved hand, and I fired the first shot.

The questioner fell at Dale's feet with a new birthmark in his temple, and his horse took off. I did likewise but for the edge of the house, and I realized it was unlikely a Snopes could go three-for-three in gunfights without some type of bad luck following. I prayed to God this was an exception to that unfair rule and sped to the cabin's edge—to defend my home.

Defend was a funny word. I was trying to not get shot, protect my folks, and maim these lowlifes, and all I could think about was action. Thoughtless action. Shoot a devil. Duck and cover. Inch around the side of the house and try to ambush more devils trying to attack our cabin. God gave me these impulses for a reason, I reckoned.

I checked my ammo, drew bead on another fellar sneaking up the porch steps, and let loose another blast of my Colt. He fell and Laverne, or one of the others, screamed inside. Ma smacked her straightaway, I imagined. Pop was probably cowering beside the lumpy mattress and praying for his whole life.

Two down. The heads weren't multiplying like those Greek myths either. Ms. Layton spoke of them once as gruesome, and I made the same face she did when she said that word *hydra*. I saw a miracle as those three vagabonds turned tail and ran after their fleeing mounts. No longer sure who was killing them off.

My fingers on my shooting hand were frozen in clawed curls around the pistol. I was a pistoleer, vulnerable because of my piece. I needed to unhook myself and make my presence known to family.

I called out, "'S me. Don't do nothin' *asinine* in there." A word I'd wanted to use since I was barely off'n the teat. Not like they'd do anything brazen enough to stop me, from entering the Snopes cabin. In I walked, happy my voice was suddenly deeper, raspier from the cold.

Pop was kneeled over the dusty, family Bible, with one eye spied on the newcomer. He didn't stand up but acted like I was a figment of his imagination. Just kept looking at some passage in the front part of the book. Ma held shaky arms out like she wanted a hug. Laverne blathered, "Told ye so, didn't I? Wouldn't hear me, though. Nope."

I tapped the Colt against the back of my neck. The cabin was warmer than anything I'd ever felt in my life. Part of me wanted to fold up and melt into the stove.

I held my gaze on this Snopes family and felt despair for them. Dale opened his mouth like he was about to jabber on about how much of a man he was, how disrespectful I'd been. But, I reared back with the still frigid, steel chamber of the Colt and knocked him against the cheek. He fell over and grabbed at his jaw and groaned, spitting a tooth, some extra onto the dirt floor.

"I won't have you disrespectin' your blood like that," Ma started in. I pointed my free, index finger up at her and shook it back and forth.

"You know what I just did, don't you? 'Cuz I don't think you do."

None of them mumbled a peep.

"Why you're still breathing and safe? Not facing judgment today? 'Cuz I do."

Pop found a little strength and stood on shaky legs. *This is his only resistance,* I thought. *Squash him now and that's that.*

"Who do you think *you* are?" his voice shook. His hand instinctively went for the belt like a marionette doing what its controller demanded. The belt was on the bedside table, and I was thankful for the little things. I swallowed and offered a steely gaze—to forever end the garbage spewing from his mouth. He inhaled, and I held up the Colt, pointing it toward his frame. Pretended like I might pull the trigger. Just said, "Pheww," and he flinched and cried out.

"It's my gun now. I didn't want it to come to this. But, I don't see a choice. You lay a hand on any of the others, Pop, and you'll find out. Ye hear?"

When Pop didn't speak, I yelled at him and he said he heard. I said good and nodded at Dale and hugged Mose briefly. I saw a new look in Mose's eyes. Like the veil had been lifted to reveal a room he'd not seen before. A life he'd never lived. One where he could smile and hug me back and not worry about a deadbeat calling him names. I told him to look after the little uns.

Before I left I scooped up all the corn pone, some jerky, and preserves that I could find. There were a few potatoes in the potato bin, too. It filled up my satchel and I felt good with the heft of it against my back. I kept it slung over my shoulder and told Mose more than once he had to stay.

But he wouldn't listen. And deep down, I knew what Pop would do to him. He'd wait until I cleared out and unleash holy hell on Mose, just to spite me and my wishes. So, as I took our lone remaining work horse, Macho, from the stable, I relented and let Mose hop behind me on the saddle blanket.

We reached the edge of our property's clearing, and Mose turned to wave to the cabin. No one waved back except Laverne. I snapped at Mose. Asked him what in tarnation he was doing.

He said, "Beats me," and laughed.

I stared at him, then turned in the saddle and smirked over my shoulder. He was right. *What else could we do?*

CHAPTER FOURTEEN

Winter was a peculiar time in eastern Kentucky. The detritus of fall became buried under snow, froze, went away, melted, and sometimes washed back into sight with the budding spring. It wasn't permanent, but it sure felt that way. Leastways until the ground was visible to the naked eye again. I liked it and I didn't. It was pretty to see the white everywhere. To walk with it crunching underfoot. To see the marks on virgin ground, as it muddied into slush and became brown like last year's forgotten things rediscovered.

"I like winter better than any other season," Mose confided, almost reading my mind.

"Why's that?"

We were now inside Ms. Layton's home. She saw us trudging up Main Street in Hazard and told us what we were up against now. What she *knew*. It was unsafe to be broadcasting our whereabouts midday, she said. Phil wanted us imprisoned as much as French wanted us stone-cold dead. Both sides of the law were after us now. Apparently, you couldn't just go around *killing folks*. It was unfitten. I saw my face on a wanted poster outside the saloon and figured she said gospel truth. So, we were inside her home now.

Ms. Layton stoked the fire with a poker, and I was more than a little glad to be back under the same roof as Maggie. I hadn't told Mose about *that* detail and didn't know if I should. Maggie was something secret. Someone I'd gladly lay it all down for like Sissy. I stared at the embers being turned over and glowing orange, red, and somewhat bluish.

"That's a good lookin' fire you got goin'," I said, trying to break the silence.

It felt like a funeral. I had my Colt tucked away. Mose beside me. Maggie was somewhere in the cavernous home. "Where's Maggie?" I asked, trying to sound offhanded about it, but Ms. Layton turned and paused shifting the coals. *And the secret's out...I worried.*

She looked at me and Mose. Smiled at the heat's source. Put the poker in its steel placeholder. Ms. Layton sat down and looked us over real good. I felt like a speech was coming. The ones Ma inhaled deeply for, before telling us something we'd done wrong. It was the same way now. Ms. Layton exhaled, "She's upstairs. Getting ready for church."

"It's Sunday already?" I asked, trying to make the conversation stretch as long as it could, before its inevitable conclusion. "I know Mose and I need to get back into the Lord's house soon. Been a few weeks since..."

Ms. Layton leaned from her chair and put her hands around my shooting hand. The gloves were hot inside the house. I should've taken them off, because I was sweating inside the leather. I reached to unwrap her grip, but it tightened.

"You know what happens next, don't you, Ezekiel?"

"It's Z," Mose offered for me.

"There are men *looking* for you. They want—"

"You mean the ones I shot? I know. We took care of them. I did leastways."

"There's a rule, Z. With outlaws, I mean. You never get *finished*. There will be more men. You best get your brother to safety." And with that she let go of my hand and left the room.

"Does that mean we ain't goin' to the Lord's house with her and Maggie?" Mose asked.

Her tone had me sweating all over. *It might not ever end. Or, end the way I wanted it to.* I felt Mose shaking my shoulder. "Z, can we go? Can we?"

He meant church, but I said yes anyways. We had to go somewhere. And fast.

CHAPTER FIFTEEN

Fult French and Phil's office were both after us now. I glimpsed Mose eyeballing my pistol. And covered up the cold gun with my undershirt. He looked over my shoulder. I grunted and kicked Macho in the withers. His ears went back. The muscled horse sped up and stumbled over Canebreak Creek.

The gun was loaded and I thought more than once about all the bumping and lurching accidentally setting it off. Blowing a hole in one of us like it had those other men. I didn't care about me as much as I did Mose. I'd already taken a small wound, but I didn't want to picture little brother with a gaping hole. I *whoae*ed on Macho and he snorted. I swatted him on the neck with the leather reins. Eventually he halted, and I dismounted.

"Stay put," I told Mose and he listened better than Macho.

He watched me like the best pupil Appalachia ever saw, and I wondered if he would make Ms. Layton a proud teacher someday. Mose's eyebrows went up and had a way of pontificating without saying a word. I always loved that about him.

"I don't want to accidentally shoot you," I answered, unloading the bullets into my coat pocket.

"We might run into them," his soft tone offered.

I looked to the forest we were traipsing into, and my heart dropped a little. He was right. I respected little brother. And I reloaded the shells and snapped the chamber shut—making sure one wasn't in the ready position. At least I could hammer it before shooting. His pale, crescent moon face agreed.

I would've loved a scout, a vanguard. But, it was just us. An army of two. I thought of Pop skirting the war betwixt the states. Kentucky picking a side. Pop staying under the quilts earlier that day, trying to wait it out. *Coward.* I wanted to call it to his face, but what was done was done. I pretended I wasn't from the same stock. I was carrying us into danger, and I felt like I was right in my actions.

Mose bounced up and down on the horse. I tried to keep Macho's path straight. The journey wasn't smooth for little brother, riding without a saddle to cushion his hind end. And, the frozen ground didn't relent much. Macho snorted and carried on like the restless beast he was.

"We'll stop up here. I found a little aperture. We can get some kindlin' and use the matches I snagged from the cabin. Get a fire goin' and eat us a bite. This cave will do. Keep us safe and dry from the elements."

Mose looked ahead, as Macho climbed. "Up there?" he pointed.

"Bingo," I said, happy for his eyesight. He'd be a handy lookout still. Someone to warn of possible threats. My vision wasn't the sharpest at night. I imagined monsters not there. Mose could keep us focused, and I thanked God for him.

"You smitten by Maggie?" Mose asked later, when we were holding cold toes and fingers to the fire I'd struck.

I stared at the flames licking together wondering how he could be so astute.

"I could tell by the way you said her name to Ms. Layton. It was your tone what gave you away."

"Aren't you sharp?" I teased back, not caring that he knew. It was nice to share the news with someone.

More snow fell outside the cave, and I watched it whiten the earth. Hazard was blanketed in purity. Mose snored lightly against the rocks with his backside to the fire. I put a few more twigs to the dwindling flame. It churned slowly to life again—eating, licking at the air.

The smoke funneled out past us into the grey sky. I imagined prayers floating to God like this. Maybe I was delirious. The smoke curled and danced on the air, and my eyes watered. Sissy always liked watching things get carried away like tree leaves from our yard, hay cut fresh from the field, and even Squeak's mane blowing on a trail ride.

Maybe I'm cursed. Everyone dies that's close to me. I looked to Mose nestled against the rocks. *I can't let him die.* I wanted God to know I couldn't. *Mose, can't die!* I cried to myself. Then, the next thing I knew I was jerking right awake, because I'd fallen asleep and no one was lookout. No one was covering our spot. I shook Mose.

I saw the fire on its last dregs puttering to death. Mose pulled his coat closer, ready for whatever. I didn't give word that we'd leave. I didn't want to boss him like Pop. I wanted it to be his mission as much as it was mine. The Snopes Brothers together.

I ran the name by him. He liked it. Said it sounded tough like we were desperadoes. I told him we weren't outlaws *but* good guys. Like Joe Eversole's clan who'd been at war with the French feudists of late, shooting the bark off every tree from Hazard to Leslie County in the name of justice. *We were Hazard's redemption,* I told him. He liked that even better and pushed his cowboy hat onto his small head. I took mine off my chest and situated it on my noggin to where my eyes were barely visible. Mose laughed.

"Bad guys don't know what hit 'em, do they, M?"

Mose perked up at the new moniker. He grinned from ear to ear and nodded his head eagerly. "Surely don't, Z."

"If we keep our heads level, we can really make 'em pay for Sissy, ye know?"

Mose said he did and started to talk about her.

I listened to his eager tale about how much Sissy used to best him at catching crawdads in Canebreak Creek.

Mose asked for a corn pone. I gave him two. Told him we needed to be strong. He flexed his bicep and offered to wrestle me. I waved him off. He was as ready as any inexperienced warrior could be. I ate jerky and spit the salty aftertaste out and swished with canteen water. Preserves on corn pone weren't bad. I had some. It was strawberry.

Mose wanted to be lookout next, and I didn't argue. The added time in the cave felt good. My cheeks were windburnt. I would rip part of my shirt and put it across my face like a bandana the next time we set off. I had to be smart, if we were going to survive other scraps with these devils.

CHAPTER SIXTEEN

Mose whistled once.

Our warning call.

I hammered back the Colt and positioned myself flush against the rocks inside the cave. Mose backed to the edge and held up his index finger like I told him—gave me a count of how many. One. *One was manageable.* A horse nickered and a rider dismounted. "That's close enough!" I barked from inside the cave. The echo gave me a nice, sonorous sound. The footsteps halted.

I inched out to almost parallel with Mose and saw a man sporting a tall hat.

If I had better eyesight I would've swore it was Lincoln himself. But, I knew he was gunned down in '65. This man removed his hat, and I saw the white hair. The preacher from the Good Counsel Church had found us. "How..."

"You two oughta be more careful about lightin' fires in winter," he said, concern in his voice.

"Did Ms. Layton give you our whereabouts?" Mose chimed in, trying his hand at being tough.

"Didn't need to, son. I saw the smoke from the church steps. It carries a mighty ways."

We hushed up at that.

"Mose hain't done a thing, preacher, honest," I pled. "He's innocent."

He just held out his hand for little brother to shake, said, "Roger."

"Why don't you help us out and stop followin' us."

"I don't need more death on my hands."

The way he said it made me wonder how many people had died because of him. He didn't say, just stared at us.

"Keep the fire out. All the way. All night long."

"We'll freeze, preach—"

"What Mose means is we do better when we have a little light to see by," I interrupted.

"I said what I said. Your call ultimately. But, French's men can track boot prints three days stale with a snowstorm in-between. They don't need any help. Phil's aren't that far off from the same skills."

"Well, I want Mose safe," I conceded, not mentioning my own neck. Roger's horse snorted, stamped its horse-shoed foot and made a loud *clomp* sound.

"Shh," Roger warned, holding his finger up. "I mean it. Not a peep." And he stuck his head out of our enclosure.

Nothing moved or stirred and Roger told us as much after a tense quarter hour searching with a brass spyglass held to his eye. He said, "I mean it. No smoke. You should prolly move out, but since the sun isn't up, stay put and leave first light."

I didn't like him telling us what to do, but I didn't have a real plan either. "What all do you know?" I heard myself ask.

"Watchmen in Hazard are set up to alert Phil if you return. You'll be arrested. Hung first thing. No trial."

"And?"

"French knows you ain't goin' away. He thought Oz's death was a fluke, but then you stopped those other boys of his, and now he's sending more. He says he don't have time to fight Eversole's faction and everybody else in eastern Kentucky. You're a bug under his heel, I've heard tell. He wants coal, and he wants every bit."

I laughed out loud suddenly, too loud, and Roger knocked me in the jaw. I winced, but I didn't react like Pop hitting me. Roger's fist was a wakeup bump. I rubbed the spot and shook my head.

"Shhhh."

"I've never had a choice, preacher. Can you understand that?"

Roger frowned his wrinkled, day old whiskers, rubbed his chin. "We always got a choice, Z. No matter the odds."

I wanted to argue some more, but I could see that Mose was spooked. He hadn't thought about the dangers really. The realest one being a man's last, dying breath. He hadn't thought of where Sissy *was*—the thin layer of ground separating us from eternity. I hugged my brother and soothed him.

"You still packin' that Colt?"

I told the preacher I was.

"Good," he said.

"Still got plenty of shells, too."

"You'll use 'em, before this is over," he confided. "Best not lose nary one."

I thanked him for the warning, for his visit.

His lip pulled up in one corner like a smirk. But it was friendly. I wished we could all just go back to the church and let our guard down. Let our guns down, too.

Roger adjusted the tall hat on his matted hair and said he prayed for our deliverance. Mose thanked him. I walked him out to his stirrup and peered into the preacher's eyes for anything else. Anything he might've withheld. Something too bleak for Mose to hear. But, he just told me Sissy was with God. To not worry about her. And giddyuped away from our makeshift camp.

We sat across the cold, unlit fire and pretended the flames were blasting our shins and knees. Mose quietly told childish jokes until I could barely keep my eyes open. He said he'd be lookout still, and I said no, no, until he relented. I felt like dead weight, and I staggered to the cave opening to stand watch. Macho raised his head. He'd lost weight just from the little time he'd been away from home. That horse was something I never wanted to see weakened. His strength somehow gave me strength when I saw his coat, his energy. I recalled the fights he gave Pop when we were in the fields. Macho was the hardest working part of our broken home.

Mose slept a deep sleep, and I rubbed my hands together to generate some circulation. It felt like I wasn't even wearing gloves. My heart was tired of hiding out. I didn't want to die, or get my brother killed. But, I needed all of this to end. I needed God to move. A woeful body wasn't meant to live in a cave. I could handle a few more hours, but I didn't think much more. As soon as I thought that, I remembered Sissy laughing and running away as I tried to tickle her once. *She was worth it.*

I dreamed Maggie ran away from me, and I tried to catch her. I was faster than her. But, for some reason I could never get her. It was a cold feeling. And, she laughed nonstop. *What was so funny?* She had to catch her breath at some point, and when she did I would catch her. But, she didn't stop. I felt a sharp pain in my lungs and was winded. Maggie put some distance between us. The laughter drove me nuts. *Don't leave!* I wanted to shout, but my mouth wouldn't open. Maggie was a blurry image joining the sky. I reached out and felt thin air. She was gone.

If Mose saw my arms outstretched and heard me jabbering like a lunatic, he didn't say anything when we both stirred. He just watched Macho eat some oats he'd sprinkled on the ground. *I have the best little brother,* I thought. *Even if Pop wants to bring him harm.* That wasn't anything new. We were used to being misfits.

CHAPTER SEVENTEEN

I heard tell from Dale once (after he came home from the schoolhouse) that Hazard was given its name after General Oliver Hazard Perry. The county, too. He was some hero of 1812. I figured he'd be rolling over in his grave if he knew what the Hazard streets were like. Mud and boards. Violence. Sad.

It hit me as odd that he fought in a war to stop another nation from conquering him, and this town in Kentucky, named after him, struggling still. I was in the thick of it. I was against Fult French and his devils. And they wanted more than the good Lord intended man to have.

I shared the jerky and pone and what was left of the strawberry preserves.

"That's it?" Mose asked.

I dusted my hands off.

"I guess we have to kill our food from here on," he added, matter of factly.

I ruffled his hair, and he told me to quit.

"I could kill a turkey if I had to," he confided, mimicked shooting the pistol in his small hand.

"I know you could."

"Or, a quail, or, a deer. I could shoot us a deer, Z."

"I know. I know you could. Hey, listen. I was thinkin' about what preacher man said. About leavin'..." I scratched my whiskers. "He means us no harm. Why else would he come out here and risk his neck to tell us? He wants us to get somewheres safe. It's not here, because we can't even light fire and stay warm without being spotted. We need to take heed and move straightaway."

Mose packed and didn't argue. I was so used to fights with Pop that it was something I prepared for always. It was beautiful to be able to pack camp and ride on without delay. Macho carried us alongside the mountain and traversed the snowfall no problem. I patted him and almost forgot about Squeak. Almost.

I knew ambush was the way villains did their bidding. It was a full proof tactic for sabotage. But, me and Mose were learned. We took this kind of plan and flipped it. We were always on the move. Never resting in one spot for more than a day or two. French's men didn't rightly know where we were laying camp from night to night. We were as shocked where our bedrolls fell as anyone else, and I loved that about our time on Shady Mountain together.

CHAPTER EIGHTEEN

Knowing how French and Eversoles' gangs first got so violent was half of knowing why we were in the trouble we were. There were a lot of rumors but the two main ones were:

-a pretty woman (and a lying store clerk) set the two parties at odds

-coal rights and greed (especially French cheating Kentuckians out of property)

I just knew what Pop and others said. These two clans were setting the whole county on edge. And I had to believe something, because my neck, and Mose's, was very much on the line.

If I ever wanted to see Maggie again, I had to fight against them. Luckily, I didn't know of anyone from the Eversole camp trying to maim us. But, it could change like the temperament of an oxen on the plow. Those wanted posters with my face on them, with fat rewards, had a way of getting results.

I wanted us hid and clear of any ambush. Mose deserved to grow to a ripe old age, and it was my job to get him there. Even if I couldn't bring back Sissy and watch her grow and marry. Mose could get there with my help. We dug in deep—far out of sight, safely away from the city—and lit a fire and searched for coney to make a stew. We didn't find anything but a few squirrels appearing from a tree knot.

I let Mose take aim and shoot his first meal. The cleaning was tedious. Their bodies were small but tasted delicious. And I admit, less gamey than a rabbit stew would've.

With our bellies full, we abandoned our bone orchard and made haste to hide again.

I heard a fuss in the snow beyond us and knew it wasn't another squirrel. We didn't even have time to dismount, before I saw a hat appear from behind a tree.

"Fetch my Colt," I said.

Mose brought it around and I told him to hold it steady on top my shoulder. He'd have to shoot this one, since we were horseback.

"What if it's Roger?" Mose cried.

"Preacher man would've announced himself," I said and told him to keep it steady.

The rider's horse snorted, and I heard, "Halloo. It's a friend. Don't shoot. I'm comin' over."

We heard him dismount, and I recognized the preacher's face. Told Mose to unhammer the gun. He fumbled with its weight, and I brought it around and did it for him.

"Heard gunfire the other day. Knew it was a Colt from the blast. Wanted to make sure you got whatever before it got you. Glad to see you're above ground. Surely I am."

"Mose got us dinner," I bragged. "He's carryin' his weight just fine," I added, looking at him on the saddle blanket behind me. I nodded and he dismounted, and I did likewise. I felt safer with the preacher nearby. I tied Macho's reins around an elm and listened to whatever our guest had to say.

Snow let up and Roger led us over to his saddle.

His horse snorted and Macho returned the favor. Beast language happening around us.

"Much better job this time," he said, winded. His Adam's apple working itself up and down as he tried to swallow.

I felt his thirst pain. Told him we could melt some snow. Get him a drink. He shook his head.

"Hidin' yerselves. But, I still found ye didn't I? And I'm no Injun scout."

I looked over at Mose, but he didn't say nothing.

"We can't just disappear, preacher," I grumbled. Not wanting our one lone visitor to badger us.

"I don't want you to die, Z. Either of you. And, I saw a big ole posse who didn't look like they planned on backing down. Whole lot of 'em in Hazard. And rumors of others in Hyden. You either wallop all of these gangs, or, make yerself so scarce no one knows yer even drawing breath. Got me?"

"I just wanted Sissy to—"

"Right. You *did*. And now they just want you dead. Trust me. They don't want to fandango. Just fetch you to the gallows. Plain and simple. I reckon you'd like to live a little while longer. Am I right?"

Mose said he did; he grabbed my hand and squeezed it.

I shook him off. "What we gotta do to get through this alive, preacher?"

"It's Roger," Mose interrupted.

Roger laughed.

I turned to my brother and gave him my best scowl. Lips frozen with eyebrows raised, I said, "Tell us what we *should* do."

"There's that urgency I was expecting. Good."

He reached into his satchel and withdrew a leather-bound Bible.

That gospel sharp wasn't ever going to quit, I thought.

He turned and said, "Hear me out."

Opening the book, he turned to a passage and stuck his finger on it. Then laughed at himself, squinting. "My glasses," he laughed, handing the heavy book to Mose.

I pushed icy air from my lungs and shifted my weight on the hillside.

"Here we are," Roger said, adjusting his spectacles and retrieving the Bible again. "All right," he cleared his throat. "Be merciful unto me, O God, be merciful unto me, for my soul trusteth in Thee. Yeah, in the shadow of Thy wings will I make my refuge until these calamities pass by." And, he snapped the book shut and handed it back to Mose, who dipped under its weight.

Roger lowered his head, "Lord, help these two to trust you. Cling to you. As hell comes after them. Be merciful as only you can. And let evil pass them so they can reach safety. Amen."

"Amen," Mose said.

I wiped my cold, dripping nose, and told him to take his Bible back.

Roger shook his head. Said we'd need it more, even though I didn't see when we'd have time to entertain scripture—bullets flying and such.

Roger leaned over and hugged us both in an awkward grip. I tried to pull away, and he let me. He gripped Mose behind the neck, and said, "Take care of your big brother. Aim true."

I was about to tell him I fired the shots, not Mose, but before I could, the preacher turned and retrieved another pistol from his satchel.

A Remington .44 model with a wooden handle, gold trigger. He handed it to Mose and said two guns were better than one out here in the sticks. He looked like he had a tear in his eye, but he quickly wiped whatever it was away.

"Don't you need your gun, Roger?" Mose asked.

"Not at the present time. You two will be needin' that. I'll be prayin' and so will our church. What's left of it. Stay up here. Climb higher. Make

French's horses climb. Phil's, too. Wear 'em down. Got me? Only use that man-stopper if need be."

I half-listened, as Mose responded to the preacher.

Roger said, "Proud to know you both," and rejoined his steed. He waved and Mose returned the gesture. I gazed at the lower reaches of the valley in Hazard's direction. The direction from whence trouble would surely come.

"What are you gonna do with that big ole book?" I asked little brother. "We can't take it with us. It's too much. It'll weigh Macho down." But, I knew how silly that sounded. I just didn't want the extra baggage.

"We have to!" he pleaded. One of the few times he ever challenged me. "Roger gave it to us. We need to listen, Z."

This time tears fell, staining his already dirty, dusty cheeks. I didn't want to see that. Didn't want to hurt him more.

"Where will you stow it?" I asked him, unreining Macho from the elm.

"I...I...I'll sit on it!" he said.

My head turned sideways a little. I wanted to hear this.

"Yeah. I'll put it like this," he modeled, trying to lift the heavy Bible above his shoulders and digging deep for strength I didn't know he had. He *thunked* it down on the blanket—causing Macho to shift nervously.

"It'll give me more height, see?" he grinned. He patted the book. "My butt won't hurt at all like it has been. It'll be better," he encouraged. "I won't have to stop so often."

That appealed to me. We needed to quit all this jawing and get up the mountain. The absence of leaves and few, covered evergreens weren't doing much in the way of hiding us.

"Fine. Fine," I relented. "Bring that whopper. Sit still, and if it gets in the way, it's gone first thing."

Mose understood and sat a full head taller, when he was in place. *It did provide a better vantage point for him as lookout.* He could see trouble before it saw us. Macho clambered up the side of Shady Mountain, higher than we'd ever been. His muscles worked overtime, and he struck a good lather.

I thought of brushing him down when we stopped. Macho couldn't take another cold, wet night. He'd catch flu. He huffed, snorted, blew hot smoke, and we leaned forward on the saddle, as much as we could, to help him crest the mountaintop. At nightfall, we reached the peak and put our bedrolls under an evergreen together.

I brushed Macho with forked sticks as best I could, since I didn't have his curry comb. He grunted when I dug too deep, and the cool air dried his sweaty back, and I tried to wipe off excess water as best I could. My leather gloves were drenched in his lather, and I took them off and hung them on tree branches beside us. "G'night, boy," I told Macho, and Mose responded with a "G'night."

I rolled over and saw Mose looking at the Bible—trying to squint his way to whatever the text said. "G'night, brother," I told him. "Don't hurt yerself. Just wait til first light to see it."

He wanted to know where it said what Roger read earlier. I didn't have the heart to tell him it was a big book. Instead, I lay my head on the hard ground and knew we were the only souls on that mountain.

CHAPTER NINETEEN

I woke in the middle of the night and my toes were frozen solid. I tried to get some circulation, but none came from rubbing them. I looked over and saw Mose staring blank-eyed. He sometimes slept that way.

"I can't feel mine either," he said.

"Have you been up this whole time? Have you slept?" I whispered.

"Not a wink," he whined. "Sss sssoo cold, Zzz."

And I knew he wouldn't complain otherwise. It had to be bad. If either of us got frostbit, that'd be the end of us. Losing a limb, or worse, in the midst of this chaos. It couldn't play out that way. I took the semi-frozen coat and raised it for Mose to get closer to me. Then, I knew it wouldn't help much, but I took the stiff-as-a-board saddle blanket and put it over top us.

"Better little brother?"

He hugged me.

I didn't fight him off. I didn't have the energy. It was important we regain strength for morning. I thought about the verse preacher man read. Mercy and trust were needed now. *God please*, I prayed into the frosty covers.

Mose slept flush against me, for a while. Until Mother Nature called me with an urgency only she could muster.

I found a spot and relieved myself. I checked to see if anything had turned blue. But, my nether regions were fine. The covers had worked.

Mose slept for another hour, and I felt bad to wake him. No new snow fell during the night, and the tracks marked our ascent plain as day. Some might mistake Roger's sorrel for ours, but it was unlikely. These weren't amateurs. At least on French's side. I couldn't attest to Phil's caliber of men.

Mose roused, and I proffered new pone and such that Roger left us. Frozen plumb through. He tried to soften them with his teeth and I did likewise. The jam didn't make it easier—gluing the two sides of each together. The jerky bits were salty and good on our sore throats. The wintry night air had us raspy-voiced like old men.

We picked up clumps of snowfall and sucked at the slushy mixture. It was tasteless and cold but did the trick. The cold temperature made my teeth chatter like I might have a rotten tooth.

"Hear anything, Z?" Mose asked.

I mumbled around the pain in my jaw that I didn't. Not a sound. *Not even a bird chirping.* We could probably hear people on another mountain with quiet like this. It was good we didn't talk above a whisper last night, I thought.

Mose retrieved the Bible and started flippin' through the pages again. "Where was that verse agin'?" he asked, trying to balance the big text on his skinny lap.

"Mose, we need to sit back-to-back and pay attention to our surroundings. Not have a study."

"I know. I just wanted to see."

"Then, you'll hush up and help?"

"Honest."

"Psalms is next to Proverbs. More chapters than any other. You should find it about midway," I pointed.

He paused in Isaiah, and I said one more past. His little fingers landed on Psalms, and I remembered the chapter Roger held open to us—one of Sissy's favorites, too. I took it and showed Mose the verse again. He mumbled the chapter and verse to himself. Then read the passage again and got real quiet.

"God is with us. So we have to be okay, don't we?" he asked. "It says so," he gestured at the verse. "Right here."

I wanted to tell Mose I was a bit more skeptical, but I knew it wouldn't help. He needed to believe, and I guessed I did to.

"Z?"

I closed the book for him, and told him, of course. *Who was I to cause my brother to worry like that?* He reopened and fiddled with the other parts of the chapter and kept quiet.

I had nothing else to do but pray for just as much. Mose believed, and I needed to. We sat watching from both sides of Shady Mountain and not a critter stirred. I wanted coffee and Mose read scripture.

It could go one of two ways, I figured: Fult French could bring Hades with him and kill us first thing, or, both French and Phil's parties would kill each other at the same time and we might perish still.

Option two looked better. From where I sat, numb and all, I wanted someone to give in. It wasn't going to be us. I remembered those I'd knocked over already, and it was just the start. Sissy was avenged. And now, it had grown. Half the town wanted me to hang for doing as I saw right.

Would they follow us forever? Well, if they took us on in the dead of winter, I could guess so. I reckoned it was a bloodlust that never slept. They were somewhere else awake longing for retribution, justice, whatever else man craved, long into the night like I was.

CHAPTER TWENTY

Rebs died and Union, too. For a cause they imagined greater than themselves. A nation divided with hate. I felt it, too. No home and no country. Fult French was trying to strip others of land. Buy 'em out of house and home. All for what sat beneath. *What were we to his gang anyway? Me and Mose?* Just two troublemakers who got in their way.

I remember Pop telling Dale at the dinner table once a little about the men French hired. Somethin' that made me smile as my butt froze to the ground. He'd said, what was it? They were *cheaply hired hands*. Some he'd said were as low as a couple dollars apiece. *Hah!* That got me fired up. Sitting there in the snow and realizing something so wondrous.

I smacked my leg too loud, and it interrupted Mose's reading. He craned his neck sideways and leaned over into my space. "Z, you see somethin' on your side?"

I grinned even bigger, and quit looking at the particulars. I turned and faced him—grabbing his cheeks. I looked at his pure, young face. No crow's feet or wrinkles yet. "Mose, guess what?"

"I want to tell you about this chapter—"

"Later," I said, waving it off. "Guess what?"

"What?"

"French's men are low-paid hires. Can you believe that?!"

"What?"

"It means a few might be good with a pistol, but most just want a quick payday. Prolly never sighted on a man and drew bead. Let alone shot one. It means you might have better aim than some of 'em!" I laughed and let go of his face.

I watched his eyes perk up. A smile formed—upper lip and bottom—showing not a few teeth. "I know I could," he said, adding confidence to the discovery. "I shot those squirrels, didn't I?"

"You sure did. Deader than doornails. And if you aim like you did then, we'll be all the better for it. Some might even flee at the first sign of trouble."

Mose agreed with a too eager nod. To an innocent bystander, we might've been haggling over grain prices. But, we weren't. This was war. And we were children no more.

I let Mose tell me about the verses in Psalms and others he flipped to. I didn't see harm since we could hear a crow squawk from miles away on top of this peak. I said Psalms was written by King David. There were songs and worship in there, some of the best, and Sissy's favorites.

"David danced," Mose laughed. "See here?"

"You're a quick reader, little brother. Who taught you how to read so good?"

"Sissy," he admitted.

I never thought he was so fast. It was like he was a sponge soaking it all in. Every little drop and morsel of verse.

"You gonna be a preacher?" I asked, but my tone was harsher than I realized. Like I was judging the cloth.

"Ain't figured yet. I will if you think it's a good idea."

I paused. What I said right then would impact him more than a little. Much like Pop lashing at us, I knew the power of words. I turned, looked from the book to Mose, and thought of Roger. Sounds of Sissy singing hymns came back to me. I missed her voice.

Heard my own squeak, "Lord works in mysterious ways..."

"I know," Mose rejoined. "Look at us up here on Shady. Anything could happen."

It most certainly could. And, I told him he'd make a fine preacher. One I'd want to come listen to.

He punched my arm, and I scruffed his noggin. We carried on like that for a while.

A crow squawked, and it brought me back to our plight. Mose closed the book, and I told him to set it aside. We needed to be swift, light of foot. He didn't argue. His vision was better than mine, and he scanned his side of the mountain. The crow squawked in that direction again, and Mose scanned the terrain.

"See anything, little brother?"

He held up his hand, and I knew that meant he did. Something was closing in on us. If it was French (or his hired outlaws), I could bet they wanted to put us down and collect the reward. Mose nudged me in the back with his elbow, "See anything on your side?"

I told him I didn't. He got my attention and I looked at where his finger pointed. Several horses made their way up and not a one with a rider we recognized. Then, Mose grabbed my shirt collar and pulled me to eye level. "See that?"

His vision was better than a hawk's!

"See what?"

"That!"

I followed his finger, and in the back of the line was a rider with a brass star. *Phil.* He was along for the trip, and I looked to Mose.

"Law wants us to turn ourselves in for murder," he said.

"Hush. You didn't kill anyone. Just me."

Mose wanted to know our play, and truth be told, so did I.

I told him to keep an eye on that group, and I scanned the other hill. *Nothing.* I did an odd thing and made a request of God. Asked him that if this was calamity, then now was as good a time as any to draw us close to His wing.

"There're halfway up," Mose said.

The lead horse paused, and I was shocked they could do that mid-climb on the steep hill. Mose told me the rear rider, Phil, was looking at them through his spyglass. *Good, he's seen us just like we've been eyein' him. Now, the cards were on the table. Ace-high to you, Phil.*

"Do you want me to shoot 'em with this?" Mose asked, raising the Remington.

I knocked it back down, out of sight from Phil's lawmen. It was loaded to the brim like Roger showed us. But, I didn't want to risk a shootout just yet.

"We could pick 'em off one at a time," Mose added, reading my mind.

We could … and we could meet the good Lord tonight, I thought.

"You have a gun now. And so do I. We shoot when *I* say."

Little brother shook his sandy brown hair, brushed it from his eyes with his non-gun hand. I smushed the cowboy hat down even further on his head.

"When do we shoot?" I asked.

"When you say," he mumbled.

"There might be a way out of this yet," I said, to calm his nerves.

I didn't have a clue what that way would be.

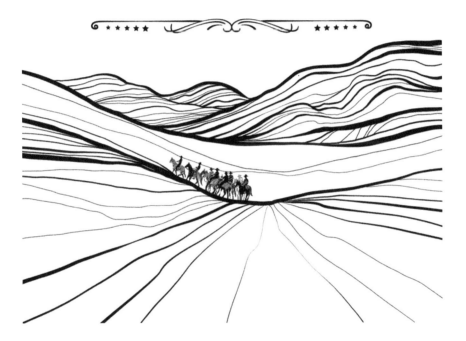

Phil's group—eight riders total, one on an Appaloosa—trudged to the mountaintop. Stopping about a hundred paces short of us.

Mose resituated his grip on the Remington, and I told him to stay calm. Keeping the gun hidden under his blanket at his leg. He listened like a good brother.

"You brought eight riders for me?" I shouted, mustering courage and remaining seated—knowing they knew we had defenses.

"You and your brother," Phil conceded. "Knew you had another in tow.

Preacher man told us so...albeit reluctantly." He grinned to the rider in the front of their group.

"You didn't hurt him, did you?" Mose piped up, anger making his limbs shake.

I said for him to shush, and Mose trembled in silence. I asked little brother's question again. They said they roughed him up a little, but he'd be able to make water in no time. I nodded slowly and told Phil to get whatever they came to do over with. I was the wanted party not Mose. I was the one who killed Oz.

Phil acted as if he hadn't heard, tossed his head back revealing a chin scar. Spat syrupy, brown tobacco on the pure, virgin snow. "You act like you're in charge, Z."

"I'm wanted, aren't I?"

"And I found you. So, I see it like you're outnumbered and outgunned. Coming down the mountain with us is your only option. Alive, I mean." He shifted in his saddle, and the leather made a noise. "You weren't too cordial the last time we had a run in. Why was that? Did I do somethin' to you?"

"You know why I went after Oz," I said, cheeks finding some blood, showing red frustration.

"I don't want your kin to get any more hurt than they have to," Phil pointed. "I brought the gang, because I wasn't sure how peaceably you were gonna make this."

I thought of Sissy trying to draw breath that fateful day. I couldn't breathe either. Like an overturned wagon lay on top of my chest and goons were telling me to get up, dust it off. I couldn't. Not like this.

"Toss those pieces to the ground over here, and stand slowly," the man at the front of Phil's pack commanded.

"These boys are state troops," Phil barked. "Under express orders of Sam Hill himself."

They're losing patience, I thought.

"Dispatched to maintain order in these parts since French and Eversole and their families can't seem to keep from killing each other. You haven't heard, I guess, since you've become a mountain lion up here. There ain't but about thirty-five folks willing to walk around in Hazard still."

I shifted in my spot, checking to see if my legs were still alive. The front rider drew his gun, and I stopped.

"Whoa whoa!" Phil said. "Don't move, Z. These boys are trigger happy with all the festivities. Don't breathe unless I say so. Okay?"

The aimed pistol made me nervous. Then, as if on cue, Phil's other riders raised their guns.

With seven pistols aimed at our heads, Phil had our attention. Mose's bony spine shook against mine, and I wished I could sing to him. Tell him to read me the story about Samson bringing down the temple. But, I kept my lips shut.

"Now," Phil instructed, "reach real slow for your pistols and toss them to us. No funny business. Got me?"

Sometimes a place had to be rebuilt from the ground up. Sodom and Gomorrah. Tower of Babel. Stuff like that. *This country, too,* I thought. I hated Phil and his gang, but I realized they were just doing what they thought was right. Kind of like me avenging Sissy. They wanted Kentucky to stand again on its own two feet. In their law books, I was part of the problem.

"Toss now!" he said more sternly.

Mose must've spooked because he did relinquish his piece. It landed with a soft hush in the snow bank.

I didn't scold him, because he was doing as told. Even in such a dire spot, I couldn't help but love his pure, God-fearing heart.

"Halfway home," Phil continued. "Z, don't make us use force. We got enough of a storm brewin' with these other vigilantes. Come on and pitch it. Now!"

The enthusiasm in his voice made it sound as if he expected me to toss my Colt alongside little brother's gun. But, I couldn't. I was too far gone to be bullied by law—right or not.

My index finger went around the trigger, and I thought of how many I could take. Definitely the one in front and maybe even Phil in the rear, before those in the middle let loose.

I felt an elbow agin' my back. "Let's go home, Z," Mose pleaded.

Rather than scare him further, I knew I needed to be the big brother. I slowly took my finger off the Colt trigger and made to toss it.

Phil was serious, and I waited for him to count one, two, and on three, when I was meant to toss my Colt, a barrage of gunfire lit up behind me, deafening my eardrums. I grabbed Mose by the sleeve and we ran for his Remington. He scooped it up and we ambled behind the snow bank. I forgot where Macho stood, and I felt sick and disoriented.

I told Mose to stay put. Hammer back on his gun. I did likewise and inched above the bank and saw a lot of red staining the white. There were bodies strewn every which way. Phil limped after his horse, and I saw a man aim at his back. Before thinking twice, I drew down on that man and shot him—clipping his ear off. He yelped and hollered.

Mose cried, head between his legs. Adrenaline was the only thing giving me a surge. The one-eared man turned and held his head. He went for his gun in the snow and I took him down with one more blast.

I didn't see anyone else, but I felt a white, hot heat rip into my shoulder like a thousand cattle branding irons and I lost the Colt, watched it land down the bank.

I started to call for Mose, but a pistol grip came down on my forehead and popped me right out.

When I came to, I was tied to a persimmon tree. I remembered Ma making persimmon pudding once; I'd helped collect the fruit.

"Where's Mose?" I asked groggily.

No response.

My head felt like a bag of lead.

The persimmon pudding hunger made my stomach hurt worse. If Mose was injured, I'd unleash hell. I tried to bite out of the ropes, get at a gun I saw laying fifteen paces away. Obviously from one of the dead men.

"Mose!" I shouted, despite the hurt it caused. I couldn't even move—tied up like I was.

"Settle down, Z," a voice soothed.

"Where is he?" I pleaded. "He better be all right, you..." I said, trying to see the man.

Phil stepped over a man he'd been stripping of ammunition. He wiped his hands off on his breeches. "Look who woke up and joined us *finally*."

"I thought you ran away," I said. Because I did. The last I saw was Phil about to be shot, but I took out the one-eared guy. And I figured the lawman got away.

"I did, but I got so far, and the guns stopped. I was alive. And, I guess I have you to thank for that. Takin' out French's man like that. All but one anyways..."

"The one who popped me over the head."

"'S right. Gave you a mighty good pump knot right there," he said, touching the spot on my forehead. I winced and shook him away.

"And Mose?"

"Still behind the bank over there. I calmed him down, but he wants to talk to you."

I looked at the rope and back to Phil. He had a sense of humor. I had to give that to the lawman.

"Could you walk him over?" I asked.

"Sure. Sure. But, I don't want you messin' with his head, Z. Got me?"

I did. And said for him to just go get him already.

Mose tripped over his own feet getting to me. He tried to take the rope off, but Phil thwarted his efforts.

"Why's he tied up, Phil?"

"You know he shot a man...men," he conceded. "Is that all right for citizens to go around doing?"

Mose looked to be mulling it over, and he said he shot squirrels. Was that okay?

"Shootin' folks is different," Phil said. "I let the hired hand of B. Fulton French tie your brother up, then I knocked him off. Made my job easier."

Mose raised his chin up; brown streaks of dirt clung to his tired face.

"I'll always be your kin. You know that, don't you?" I said.

He cried into his shirtsleeve and went to find Macho in the woods.

I yelled after Mose to not veer far. Trouble might still be around. Phil said he didn't think so.

"Did French show up with them?" I asked, hanging my head.

"There were so many shots fired at once, I couldn't sort out where the devils were firing from, but as their shots hit my men in front. I saw their gunmen. French wasn't there. He knows what Kentucky law wants to do with him. No. His ratty crew were shooting up the woods, and I doubled back and tried to offer another ambush. Your shots were appreciated, too," he conceded. "I'm surprised you didn't die."

Me, too, I thought. *With that many shots fired so close?* Then, I saw the purple-red stain and mangled mixture of fabric and skin and remembered the shot. Phil winced for me, said, "Yeah. That's going to get worse before it gets better. You need Doc Branson for that."

Hearing his name made the pain worse. I really didn't want to go under the knife again with the bonesaw, but I didn't want to lose a limb either. *Whatever*, I reasoned. At least he was familiar.

"When do we start?" I asked, expecting him to delay us, to watch me squirm. But he didn't.

Phil leaned in close and told me to grab hold of him, when the taut rope was cut. I did and collapsed nicely onto his shoulder. He led me to Macho and secured me on the horse. I told him I could ride downhill as good as anybody. Mose did as told and rode alone on Phil's steed with his Bible tucked securely under his seat.

The descent felt like a million years. Every step Macho took and stumbled slightly on a wet stone, or, uneven hole, made my entire body lurch and constrict. My shoulder felt like it might need to come off. I imagined showing Bonesaw the damage this time and saying, "Take it off, Doc. Make me lopsided."

The horses led us painfully to the bottom of Shady Mountain and across the ravine and over frozen Canebreak Creek and back into city limits.

Despite all the bloodshed, it warmed my heart knowing Maggie was part of the town. Maggie and her mom. Such fine folk. And preacher man, Roger—Mose's hero. Mose, who checked on me every other step, the best little brother. Then, I thought of our Snope cabin beside Sumner Place. A family that never came to town, never relied on anyone.

Phil helped Mose dismount. Then, he helped me and reined his sorrel and Macho both to the same post. I wanted to tell him Macho didn't do so well around other horses, but I couldn't find the words. I figured he'd find out soon enough. I let him lead me into the station where my sentencing awaited. Mose held my hand and I had to tell him prisoners weren't supposed to be coddled.

He asked Phil to let me go repeatedly. I told both to forget the bonesaw. I would mend it myself. Phil relented and didn't say another word.

I went into a cell and the metal bars clanked and locked behind me. Mose stuck his hand through and told me to be patient. Like he was the parent. I wanted to tell him I had been patient as long as I could stand. Sissy demanded more.

Phil asked if I regretted what I'd done. I said no and I'd do it again willingly. Phil urged Mose to the front door.

I couldn't sleep and couldn't dream, and I wanted both desperately. All I could lock onto was a vision of the gallows in Hazard. Dale used to talk about the hanging platform. How high off the ground it was. The type of wood it was made with. How solid and secure. How long a body kicked and squirmed before the neck fully snapped.

Hazard mostly talked about outlaws that way, and I didn't think my name should be etched in hell the same as theirs. I guess I didn't think my sins were the same. I didn't kill in cold blood. *Did I?*

Who was I asking?

God?

God.

You know my every thought.

You know the numbers of hairs on my head.

Did I?

You keep your eyes on the sparrow.

Don't you?

You keep your eyes on Sissy.

Can you see her?

Can you keep Mose safe?

Can you?

I could see my sentence going a few different ways:

-I hang and my neck breaks

-I struggle and suffocate eventually

-The rope breaks and I escape

Only none of those things happened to me. For once, a bit of good luck came my way. It seemed the Snopes curse was lifted...

CHAPTER TWENTY-ONE

1 year later
November 1889
I built a ramshackle cabin alongside Canebreak Creek for Mose and me. We got on just fine after the night I spent in jail. At least at first. Bonesaw healed me again, albeit begrudgingly. Mose took to studying scripture like a good student of the Lord. I courted Maggie a lil bit, but it was tough on her.

Being the only girl her age living in a town such as the one we had. More than a few heathens approached our cabin, too. Word was I still had blood on my hands.

Phil let me go, and it shocked me more than it would've Judas Iscariot. I waited out that night in the cell, and he came first light and sprung me just like that. I started to raise questions, but he held up his hand. Told me he was getting out of dodge and for us to do likewise. Find a spot out of county and lay lower than a salamander.

I laughed, but he was serious. I was haunted by his blank stare. He said, "Don't laugh. Those Kentucky troops were just the start, Z. Just you wait and see, if you're dumb enough to stay here..."

I told him I was plenty dumb, and he didn't argue. He spun his sorrel, adding, "Besides, you saved me on Shady Mountain, and I guess this is me lettin' you live a few more days."

He rode off without so much as *Adios*.

The cabin took some effort to build. I wasn't a faller and Mose could barely carry his own weight. We built as soon as things melted and dried up. Mose did manage to shoot an elk once and we used every bit to put some of the weight back on we'd lost. Elk tasted better than anything I'd ever had. Even the jerky was delicious.

Mose read aloud from the New Testament and I carried cedar. Chopped, notched, and wedged the pieces together. It was slow going, but at least it came together for us to have something to call our own. After wintering at the church with Roger, I was eager to rest somewhere away from all the killings.

Little brother agreed. The slim numbers made Hazard feel like a ghost town. It made a body want to winter year-round in the woods. The gunfire was ceaseless.

Maggie dropped by during the cabin's construction and brought salt pork and molasses. She said it was heavenly together. I didn't believe her, although, she didn't look like she could be wrong about much. Her hair was past her waist. Tied in pigtails, braided. She squinted a little like she wore glasses, but it made her nose all the cuter. She reached for my hand and put a bit of salt pork in it.

I'd never had it without biscuits before, and I was about to ask if she had some in that basket when she brought the molasses jar out and took the lid off. She said, "You dunk it, just like this. Salty and sweet."

I stared at her and the mess the molasses made going down the side of the jar. She made me want to try it, at least. And so I dipped the salt pork with molasses and brought it to my lips. It was unlike anything I'd had before.

Maggie hung around long enough to watch the logs go into place and helped us make sure they were flush and wind resistant. I tried to get the best ones I could find. Roger came out and helped with the sawing. I didn't dare ask Dale or Pop for help. Didn't know if they were even still breathing life after that one night I saved them. But, I figured they was.

The cabin kept us cool through summer, leading into fall. The leaves fell onto the roof and into the creek bed behind. It was pretty enough to take a picture, Maggie said.

She was so sweet one day, I couldn't help but lean over and kiss her soft, pouty lips. She let me, too.

Later Mose told me she looked Cherokee, and I told him to not talk about her. But, I could see the resemblance now that he'd said it.

The next time she asked me why I was staring so.

I admitted it was her Cherokee tone, her squinty eyes. "You're the sweetest gal in Kentucky hands down."

She smiled, then her face flattened. "I'm about the only one left."

"It's a compliment," I said, going for her hand.

She let me. So, I stopped working on the porch steps, and I sat with her and talked about us. Our folks. Whether her extended kin was coming back. She thought not. Whether I was ever gonna make amends with my family. I thought not. If Mose was gonna learn after Roger in the church house. I said he was come winter again. She looked toward the creek, and I traced my calloused fingers around her soft palm, studying the tender veins.

The house saw a few more visits from Maggie and her basket, in late summer. One time we even sat and brought up marriage. She flinched a lil. But she and I was fourteen apiece now. We could get her mom's blessing and Roger would marry us. But, it was only brought up the once, as things escalated in town to the worst they'd ever been. It became even too dangerous for her to stop over. No one went outside more than they had to—what, with all the shootings.

It was hard enough courting without the risk of death. Being shot was something I was already familiar with. I didn't want to put Maggie in harm's way. Now, we couldn't even see each other. Gunshots happened and word got around county that Phil had been injured in a skirmish from siding with the Eversoles.

All this foolishness over coal and greed was just plain dumb. I mean, I didn't shoot Pop because he was a sorry animal, or Dale, for wanting to be just like him. We didn't fix our anger, *but* we left it be. They lived over there, and we lived here. Simple math, I thought.

Mose read about wars and tribulations in the Bible and told me our home wasn't too different to those in the deserts of the Old Testament. Nineveh had its problems and Jonah did before he got there and after. The good Lord knew Job had his issues. Even his wife telling him to curse God and die. But, they overcame and I figured we could as well. Somehow. One day at a time.

But, it was November now. The gunshots went off non-stop. Mose covered his ears, because they made him lose his place in Ecclesiastes, and he trembled. I thought of Maggie every time the guns sounded like they came from her part of town. We were just far enough away to catch the sounds.

"What if it comes over here?"

"We do what we did on Shady Mountain."

"I didn't do anything on Shady," Mose admitted.

Without Maggie, the cabin seemed colder. Forties and below made me think of last year. I cringed, as I thought about my Colt in a holster Phil gave me. I didn't want to use it again. Practice or no.

Mose told me I should practice, in case those gunmen stepped over our way. I thought, *Great! Here's a soon-to-be preacher and holy roller. Giving me advice.* But, I didn't argue. He was right. I wasn't much good if I couldn't clear my holster in time. French, or someone, would shoot me dead.

Mose asked when we'd start building fires again. I said we didn't stop them that long ago. And even though we had spring and summer, it still felt like winter ran year-round.

"Do you want to use your lumberjack skills?" I teased.

He sat down his journal—filled with his long notes about Saul's transformation on Damascus Road. "You mean it?"

I regretted bringing it up straightaway. Stomped my boot down on the hard, already hardening ground of the cabin. Looking squarely at Mose's youthful face, "Sure," I muttered. Then, I peered outside and scanned the skies for any sign of bad weather. Anything to deflect Mose. But, the skies were clear.

"I'll do as you tell," Mose proffered. "It's gettin' fairly dark, we best move if we want to bring in some today?"

I felt like he was telling me more than asking but he was right. Dipping temperatures weren't fun for no man. We'd sleep better with a lil heat. Maybe some hot water for tea.

Mose came outside and I said, "Let's chop up one of these we have left over from the cabin."

I had kept a few for just *that* reason—winter.

After instructing Mose and showing him the first three blocks I split, I thought he could chop a few hisself. Yet, no matter how many times he watched and clipped with the axe, he still couldn't get it. Didn't have the upper-body strength. The axe almost fell behind his head to the ground each swing. I watched him heave, grunt, barely chipping the log time and time again. It was hard to watch, but I wanted him to end on a good note.

When there wasn't one, I figured I'd help him finish the log. He was a lil downtrodden but he agreed to help me carry it to the porch. We stacked it in layers and built a wall to burn later. I thought about how good it was to have the cabin finished.

"Good thing I'm studyin' to preach, huh?" Mose whined, more than laughed. "I guess some aren't meant to be woodsmen."

"Most can't talk in fancy speeches to save their lives, but you can," I soothed. "God built you for that."

He nodded in agreement but looked at the pile of firewood longingly.

"We'll stay warm no matter who chops it, huh?"

He picked up his notes and re-read what he'd written earlier. Then he clasped his hands and seemed to be praying for something whether it was chopping skills or else I don't know. He stayed hunched over for a good bit.

I took the first few fruits of our labor and got the fireplace going good inside. The wood burned nicely and gave a favorable scent to our already pleasant cedar abode. Mose soon fell asleep with his hands clasped together.

I sat down a kettle and steeped a little tea for the night.

CHAPTER TWENTY-TWO

Gunshots increased. I soothed Mose when they brought tears to his eyes. He read verses and I admitted it helped in the shorter, drearier days. November brought rain, brushfires. The volley of gun fire from the warring French and Eversole parties didn't help the mood of our forever fractured town.

Ms. Layton pecked on our cabin door the next morning. She said they were clearing out.

"It's the only sensible thing to do now, *Ezekiel*."

Her formal tone threw me off. I wasn't used to being called by my name, and I felt mocked. I asked if that included Maggie. She said it did. They were to leave at first light. Wanted to let me know we should do likewise. I said thanks and kindly shut the door.

The going was definitely rough, but it wasn't time to cash in. *We might as well wave a white flag.* Hazard was all I knew. I didn't see how running away from everything would be best. But the echoing gun blasts made it enticing.

And sweet Maggie (with those eyes and smooth skin) leaving without a goodbye didn't help. I really would marry her, if she let me. But, her mom ushering her away was not good news. She was the only girl my age in all of the hollers and a near perfect one at that.

I couldn't sleep that night after Ms. Layton left. Maggie gone would be like never knowing her. It would be Mose and me against whatever ill fell into our yard next.

Our rooster, Nicodemus, crowed not long after my nightmare visit from Ms. Layton. He stirred me to the front door, and I saw a shadow hovering on the porch. It was hard to make out the body. Apparition or not. It brought its fist to the wooden door and rapped lightly. I opened, shocking the person outside.

"Who goes there?" I croaked.

"Z?"

I knew that sweet lilt better than my own name.

"Z, I had to say goodb—"

"Maggie, come here," I said, recognizing her now, grabbing her in a hug. "I thought you were gone away."

She breathed me in, and I planted a kiss on her lips—leaving us both breathless.

"Momma doesn't know I slipped out. We're leavin' in an hour to go to western Kentucky. Past Mammoth Cave she said."

"You could stay with us. I could keep you safe."

"Momma..."

"I could take care of you both. We have plenty of room. I could hunt deer. And Mose could read you verses. I—"

Maggie hugged me again. Kissed me with my mouth open. Then, she looked me fully in the eyes. I tried to see her better in the peekaboo darkness. But, as quickly as she held me she pulled away. The space where she stood was empty. I heard the floorboards creak, but I couldn't see her go. Just the shadow again—receding into the woods.

"What's goin' on?" I heard Mose ask.

"Maggie came to say 'Goodbye'…" I said, unsure if I believed the words myself.

"The Laytons are leavin', too? That's just thirty-three of us now, Z. What'll we do?"

"You need to pray for us to not die," I snapped, aware of how much her leaving meant to me.

I breathed in the cool, fall air and felt it weigh down my lungs, heart, whatever was still beneath. With Maggie gone, I didn't see how eastern Kentucky would ever recover. I checked to make sure the Colt was loaded.

CHAPTER TWENTY-THREE

In mid-November, news of another scuffle came from a peculiar place—Preacher Dooley. He showed up on the front porch where Maggie stood just days prior. Dooley said he brought bad tidings, more war on the horizon. I told him to say his peace and leave. Mose nudged me.

"Lil brother wants to hear ye," I muttered, beneath clenched teeth. "So out with it."

Dooley bore into Mose with his beady eyes. Got close enough so that even I could smell his stale, cow's milk breath. He exhaled, said, "Eversole's gang wants revenge on account of Joe Eversole being kilt by those French feudists. They mean business, to anyone in sight. Friend and foe. If I was you I'd make sure you and Mose git free of Perry County before the whole lot burns down the county. Got me?"

"How would a preacher know about these doings?" I pried, arms crossed.

Mose nudged me again. Tried to urge Dooley inside our cabin.

But I didn't clear the path. "Let him say his piece and git. I don't take kindly to anyone so deep in the pockets of others."

Dooley scoffed, looked outside to see if any phantom churchgoer had heard.

"I only took money that *one* time," he whispered, hands held up.

"Tell God. Not us. We don't have to answer for sticky hands," I added, closing the door.

Mose tried to allow the preacher inside again, but I fought him and closed the door with force—shaking the cabin.

"Least let me stay with you til first light," the preacher whined through the door. "That way *I* won't be in town."

"Not my problem. You can sleep on the porch, if you'd like."

No answer. Then, eventually the retreating sounds of Dooley's small boots on the planks. He left but headed away from the direction of town, I noticed.

"You could've been nicer."

"I could've let him rob us blind, too."

"He's a sinner just like any of us," Mose defended.

"But, he's expected to be a man of the cloth. Not livin' in sin. I won't stand for an unreformed preacher."

"So, you just pitch him to the wolves?"

"He'll be fine. At least he'll be if he listens to his own words."

"Where'll he go?"

"Looked like he went west. Away from Hazard. He'll be fine."

"How do you know?"

"He's skilled at lookin' out for his own hide. Cowards live longer than anyone else. I imagine he'll live to be a ripe, old miserable age."

"What about us? What if what Preacher Dooley said is true about the feuds?"

"What about it?!" I snapped. "I'm goin' to see to it that Hazard stands long after these louts have had their war. If they want to fight and bleed all winter, I'm not budging an inch. We'll stay here until the calvary joins us."

Mose shook his head. "So you'd risk it all? Haven't you heard me readin'?"

The wind pushed against the cabin logs and brought cold air through the cracks. Mose bundled tighter under a blanket. His shoulders shook. "We can't hole up here all winter without supplies. It's too much, Z."

"Our cabin will hold. Trust me. This is our home now, our land. Two families aren't goin' to run us off. What do you think God wants, Mose? Us to fold? Run away like scared foxes? No. If the Civil War didn't uproot us Snopes from these hills, no clan feud is doin' it."

"Pride goeth before destruction," Mose quoted. "Proverbs. The wisest man ever alive said that. Shouldn't we listen?"

"I'm not lookin' for trouble, lil brother. Just wantin' to keep our plot of land. See you get to preach someday to someone other than me. I aim to look out for us."

I was settled on the matter and went outside to chop more firewood, even though it wasn't needed. The wind whipped at my earlobes, and I heard high-pitched rifle shots echoing above the tree line.

How could lawlessness go so unchecked? I thought of Pop licking me on the backs of my legs with his belt. The sting felt like the threat of living in town. *I'll stop by and see for myself. I'll deal with these boys,* I thought. *I'm tired of it!*

If war was the answer to the age-old question of how to live in peace, then I'd make sure we deserved it as much as anybody. If Dale and Pop were too sorry to fight back, I would again. Just like on Shady Mountain. I was ready to give my life for this to be over.

The cold air bit at my nose and brought water to my eyes. I shielded my face with my shirt. I was about to chop another unnecessary block, when Mose waved for me to come to the porch. I shook my head, but he waved all the more frantically. I wanted to scold him. Tell him to get a grip. But, his face dropped, and I could tell it was serious.

Dooley hadn't gone west. Not straight away, Mose said, voice shaky. He'd circled behind our cabin and waited. He rapped on the back of the cabin and told Mose what was really going down in Hazard. The attack at the courthouse. Laid it all out nice and tragic. And it was too forthright on Dooley's part, to be anything but the truth. And the real kicker, Dooley had said, was who had joined the Eversoles—none other than our big brother, Dale Snopes. *That treacherous devil!*

I shook my head. Asked Mose to go over that last bit again.

Dale, our own flesh and blood, was running with the Eversoles, he repeated.

What in the heck would Dale want in a fight like this? Didn't he know this was as good as hanging himself?

But, I didn't say any of it. I kept it inside. Thought of the specifics. The courthouse. It was about noon, according to the sun in the sky, high above our heads and the cabin.

Mose wanted to talk this thing to death, but I held up a hand. "Lil brother, I'm goin' to do my part," I said, voice firm. "You can stay and read and pray for me, or, you can bring your Remington. Either way, I intend to make Perry County safer. Honest to God, I do. Even if it means we have one less brother in these parts today."

And I left the cabin and saddled Macho taut and headed for town. The

Colt was loaded and so was the Remington. Mose offered to go, but I really wanted him safe. His future was too bright. He was this holler's soon-to-be Bible man. The bringer of good news. Not death and gunfire. I wanted him to play a different part and eventually he relented—letting go of the saddle horn and me with it. Macho crunched the hard-packed ground with his feisty hooves. All was quiet except for him, as we rode over the hills and stirred up not just a little noise.

CHAPTER TWENTY-FOUR

I thought of what people said about the Civil War. The sounds of the drums and bugles as the veterans marched down Main Street.

It felt like a play rather than a ceremony. Where men and boys dressed up in uniform and went to act out parts predetermined. Like lines in a skit already formed. Now, I felt a similar way. *Were we doing exactly what we knew we would? Killing each other over stupid things like coal?* It seemed so, because it was so. French and Eversole were just names recently attached to it. Really it felt like all of us.

Except for Mose. He was pure. His heart was good. And Maggie. Maggie, yes. She was pure. Her mom, Ms. Layton, and Roger, too. There were good people left. I needed to remember that. All hope was not lost. Not yet leastways.

The courthouse came into view. I crested a final hill and Macho and me made our descent into the valley of what used to be Main Street. We passed the goods and supplies stores and saloon, and it felt it'd been years since we'd fled Hazard's city limits, not mere months. The city was in a sad state. The buildings worn beyond their years. The bricks were holey from gunfire and lead.

Even the buildings weren't safe, I laughed and caught my breath in the November chill. The street was deserted and I wondered if the courthouse would be as well. According to what Preacher Dooley said to Mose, it sounded like the next full-fledged war would soon break out. It might be another Antietam, but I prayed not.

Deep down, I didn't want to be tough. I just felt I had to. *Who else would stand against such lawlessness?*

Macho snorted and I hushed him. I tied him to the hitching post at the saloon. The same I remember latching Squeak to not long ago. My heart jumped a little at the memory. My forehead broke out in a sweat.

I walked the rest of the way to the courthouse. It gave me a better feeling to see the ground myself—on my own two feet. The Colt and

Remington were my only supporters, knocking at my waist as I approached the building. It was empty save for the judge. A different judge to the one I was used to seeing; he said his name was Judge Bigelow. He held the door for me, but I shook my head *no*. Said I'd be along shortly. This judge seemed more nervous than those accused of heinous crimes. I figured it made sense. The way our city numbers had dwindled. We went through people quicker than General Lee. No, I'd hang around and wait for others to file inside. And they did. Hired hands by the looks of them.

Ever since Joe Eversole was shot, tensions ran high. And more people were hired to make sure French didn't try to swindle them out of their lands. These men looked to be hell-bent on maintaining rights to whatever was theirs. Nothing was going to chance. And as body after body filed in, and the judge acknowledged them with a curt nod, the courthouse went from cool to stuffy too fast. But, I didn't inch in. Not yet. I stayed in the fringes.

I was a bystander, a victim, to their hatred. I wanted it *all* to be over. I wanted both parties to give in and throw up their hands and leave it in the dust. But, I knew gunfire was the only solution to such stubbornness. I carried twice the firepower on me this time. And even better, I wasn't the *wanted* party. They wanted to kill each other.

So I set up shop outside the courthouse and watched the judge get things started. I felt a flurry or two dust across my face. It was about four o'clock, I overheard one man say. I counted fifteen or so men in there with George Eversole, the one taking over his family clan now, since Joe was dead. I cheered for them a lil bit, even though I hated the killing altogether. At least they didn't stand for French swindling them out of land. Sissy would like them a tad more, I thought.

As Judge Bigelow mumbled about the large numbers coming out under bond, it clicked for me. Most were needed there in the courthouse. *How convenient!* The judge kept glancing at his watch, and I didn't dare amble back inside. The door was propped open by a do-gooder in the back row, and I was much obliged. I tipped my hat to the lady and wondered did she know how dangerous it was.

A few more unfamiliars sidled around my spot on the walkway and into the open courthouse. I saw them standing with their arms crossed in the far corners of the room. Judge Bigelow laughed nervous-like about needing to end the proceedings so he could get back to Wolfe County. His wife had supper waiting on the table.

Guns were positioned inside each Eversole fighters' belts so that even I could tell they were armed to the teeth. Only a few of French's men were present at the hearing. They gulped, swallowed every time an Eversole man shifted stance. But, they didn't run. Their eyes were fixed on Judge Bigelow, as he bumbled along about justice and order and safety.

One man of French's finally stood and held up his hand for the judge to stop. Bigelow's mouth shut like a trap. The man put his hands beneath suspenders and pulled on them and rocked on his heels.

"We have backup in the hills, in case any Eversole is wondering. So don't count your chickens before they hatch," he said, laughing and smacking the leg of the man next to him. The awkward sound of laughter in such a tense room fell flat.

If French was outside of town, it was intentional. The numbers weren't looking too good for his crew by my estimation. And I saw a few bits of movement beyond the courthouse near the jailor's residence. I couldn't see clearly, but I felt something was off. It didn't take my figuring long, because I heard a gun blast and then chaos followed.

Benches screeched and boots clacked on the courthouse floor, as men tried to wrestle their way outside. Paying no mind to the judge and his proceedings. Men flew every which way and it was all I could do to get behind a hitching post, letting the heathens lope off in the direction of the shots.

I didn't see anybody stationed on the jailor's front porch, but I saw gun blasts from a neighboring cabin. Then I thought I saw someone in the doorway of the jailor's place. From what we'd heard courtesy of Preacher Dooley, the man looked to be Bad Tom Smith—the ruthless fighter on the French side.

The groups shot at one another across the street for a good while, and I didn't leave my spot. Not yet. *Why should I?* I didn't want to die in the crosshairs of their foolishness. *Who would take care of Mose then?* No, I sat and watched and it died out soon enough. Maybe fifteen minutes or so, and the gun smoke settled down.

A body was hauled out of the cabin across the street and covered up. One of French's men by the looks of it. I tried to take stock but the groups were getting away from me, getting commingled.

Just as I spun to clear the courthouse steps, a man hustled by the building and muttered, "Come back at night, hah! Who do they think these boys are? Amateurs? French will only be stronger by then."

He wore a grimace and there was blood on his shirt. He was the one who'd cleared the body to the street.

If they were waiting 'til dark to resume, so would I. Mose would know to wait, keep the lamp lit for me. This was war. Family pitted against family. The shortened fall days promised an early nightfall. There were killings ahead of us. Justice to dole out. Sissy would want to see this thing finished.

I saw men scrambling for better position within both parties. The judge joined me near the saloon and said he wanted to leave, but it was too dark. He needed to be here for tomorrow's proceedings anyway—to complete what was left unfinished. As he spoke, I half listened and felt disdain for the law. Maybe for sending someone like Judge Bigelow to handle court proceedings. Weak. Soft spoken.

I told him to take cover. It was about to get interesting, and he scoffed at me. Said I was too young to be meddling in grown men's scrabbles. I said I'd been in such places since Pop first came down on me with his belt. The judge looked past me and *hmmphed* his way to the whiskey stool.

Part of me wanted to high tail it home. A large part did. Mose would be worried. Praying with his skinny wrists to the Lord. I missed supper and felt it in my belly.

Mr. Johnson, the barkeep, let me enter the saloon and proferred a glass of something without me asking. I saw Judge Bigelow and kept my distance.

The hours ticked by slower than anything and only an evening girl or two mingled on the top balcony looking for nonexistent business. I kept my eyes down as best I could. My stubble came in better than it did the year before, and I felt it hid my appearance somewhat. One girl waggled her finger, trying to get my attention. I focused on the amber colored liquid in my glass and Sissy. Sweet. Pure. Worth all of it.

The girl lost interest and moved to Bigelow—a judge. I almost laughed when he ambled up the stairs like a raccoon after a pat of butter. *There's justice!* I thought. I kicked back the remaining whiskey and my throat lit on fire. I coughed a big fit and someone smacked my back. I jumped from my stool with both pistols raised, and the man eased off. He was the only other soul in the bar now, apart from Mr. Johnson.

"Just tryin' to hep ye," he said. He looked about my age, but I couldn't tell who he was. He nodded and put his hands at his sides. Eventually I relinquished my grip on the guns and stowed them.

"Can't go around slappin' folks you don't know," I said, tough voiced, lowered deep. "Not in Hazard leastways."

"God's honest truth," he laughed, accidentally slapping at me again.

I pulled away.

"This place is nervouser than a long-tailed cat in a room full of rockin' chairs," he said.

I stared at him quarely. "I'm Z."

"Pickle Steeves," the young man said, extending a hand.

I shook it and started to open my mouth.

"I know. Pickle. Go ahead and say yer piece. I ate a lot of 'em when I was small. In Wolfe County. Folks loved to tease," he admitted, lowering his voice. "Nickname kinda stuck."

Again, I stared. *This boy ain't right*, I thought. *But who was?*

"What about ye? Got any special talents?" he asked.

"Judge Bigelow upstairs," I pointed, ignoring him, his question, "he's from Wolfe, too. Any kin?"

Pickle glanced upstairs. "Uncle. I came here as his *security*," he grinned. "What's your story?"

"Story? I'm pretty good with a pistol," I said. And it felt good coming out with a truth about something for once.

"A pistoleer in our midst," Pickle announced to the room. "Mr. Johnson, fetch this skilled assassin another drink!"

I held up my hand. Shook Mr. Johnson away, but he was already filling up my glass with another.

"I didn't say I was no assassin," I corrected, feeling the whiskey already.

"What's a pistoleer shoot at, if not folks needin' kilt?" Pickle surmised.

"I shoot at things along the fencerow at our place. Snakes needin' worked over."

"Never a man?"

I looked out the saloon doors over my shoulder. Not my favorite subject.

"Listen, we can talk about other things..."

"I've shot men," I admitted. "Not proud of it, but it needed to be done."

Pickle leaned in with salty, stale cigarillo breath and told me it was a man named Campbell laying in the street—one of French's bunch. He smacked the bar and said Eversole's number was now stronger; they should be attacking already.

"I hear tell French is just sittin' up in the woods outside Hazard. Watchin' us. Bringin' in more men for later. For darkness to fall. Fult French is a coward and a murderer all at once," Pickle stammered, slamming back another shot. "We have him if we take him right now. But, I'm not the one callin' it. I'm just...Pickle Steeves. Here for my puny uncle," he said. "Some story."

I crunched the numbers in my head. He was right. They were stronger now than I'd ever seen them. Hazard looked busy with so many Eversole loyalists roaming the streets. It felt lively on Main for the first time in a long while. Not considering a man had just been shot and was laying covered up outside.

"Why you risking your neck, Z?" Pickle asked, above the grunting, creaking sounds coming from the second floor.

Yeah, why was I? Sissy was avenged. I didn't live at home. Me and Mose had a place now. It felt odd for someone to ask that. So, I shrugged.

"What about you, Pickle? There must a reason you're tagging along. Willin' to play bodyguard against French's men for Judge Bigelow..."

"Unc says jump and I say how high. Plus, he pays me pretty good," he said, tapping his pocket. "I'm done with the ignorance, too. Ain't you?"

I said I was and offered to cover his next round. He didn't resist much and Mr. Johnson plunked another mug down on the bar. Pickle reached for it and holding it high said, "To my new compadre, Z, for showing me around Hazard." He gulped the drink down and smacked the mug against the wooden bar.

Mr. Johnson told him it was his last fill-up, and I didn't think Pickle could hold much more. Besides, it was getting darker still outside, and the creaking spring sounds lulled us into quieter realms.

I held my lukewarm glass, and the empty bar echoed with every glass Mr. Johnson stacked. Pickle yawned and cracked his knuckles. The room fell silent like a wake.

"Won't be too much longer now," Pickle said absentmindedly, scratching his stubble on his narrow, pallid cheeks. "French only attacks when he's got the edge, I've heard. Even darkness plays by his rules...And he's got Bad Tom, too."

"What do you mean darkness plays by *his* rules?"

"You ever hear tell of Frenchie losin' more than a couple men?"

I hadn't.

I stood and walked over to the edge of the saloon—peered out into the street. Saw a man clanking down main with spurs *kish kishing* as he went. It looked to be someone familiar, judging by the way he walked, I thought it was E.C. Morgan but I knew the Eversole party had taken care of him. As he got closer, I could tell I was close.

It was Jesse Morgan, E.C.'s brother. Fighting to avenge E.C. the way I was Sissy.

Vengeance drove most of us. Some to better ends than others. Jesse wanted justice the same way I did, but his malice was fresh. Mine was stale. Sissy would want me to turn the other cheek. I knew that now. *So, why couldn't I give it up? Let Macho roam free in the hillsides? What was I hoping to accomplish?*

Jesse made his way past the saloon, and I ducked back inside—sat with Pickle, and tapped the bar for a ginger ale. Something sweet.

"Don't got those," Mr. Johnson bellowed.

I asked Pickle if he had a deck of cards, and he said he did. We barely had time to shuffle and deal before gunfire commenced, and I knew we wouldn't be playing cards after all.

CHAPTER TWENTY-FIVE

Jesse called out for the Eversoles to stop being such yellowbellies and fight him like a man. Not hide in the bushes like snakes. Eventually, the Davidson boys did. They fired pistols at Jesse, and horses whinnied. Me and Pickle watched from the saloon doors, unsure if this was the moment to go in guns ablaze. We didn't move, and I guessed it wasn't.

Mr. Johnson gave it up and went upstairs to lock his bedroom door, carouse with the ladies. I was glad he left, stopped cleaning the same whiskey glass over and over again. Pickle pointed to a clock I'd not noticed—covered with dirt, years of cigar smoke. I squinted to see the hour.

"The clock," he said again, nudging me. I didn't like being nudged, but I could ascertain his meaning.

It read just past midnight on the tired dials—if they were right. Before I could ask, Pickle said they were.

Then, we heard Jesse yelling, "French is here! Oh boy, we got 'em licked now. You hear that Eversoles, everyone? We got yer sorry hides now!" Followed by more gunfire.

Could they make anyone out in them bushes anyways? I wondered. It was so dark just past the lantern lit street. I could hardly see outside the saloon.

"Git!" I heard Mr. Johnson order from upstairs. "I don't want the fight in here, boys!"

French's arrival made my blood boil. And my hands shook. The one I wanted the most to pay for making such a mess. Our family was already busted, but I put a lot of it on B. Fulton French. He represented evil lurking in these hills. Buying land from families, giving them next to nothing, and profiteering from the fool's gold beneath. I wanted to spit in his face.

"Who you gonna shoot first?" Pickled asked through slurred speech, like it was a drinking game.

I could tell he was sober enough. I didn't care if Jesse Morgan, and others were with French or not. French was priority number one for me.

Haphazard warning shots blasted throughout the night. I couldn't place where a volley connected with someone's flesh or missed. There wasn't a lot of hollering. Not the anguished kind leastways. Most of it was bravado. Showing off with gunpowder.

The Eversoles returned French's taunts with exclamations asking where he'd been this whole time. Pickle said he'd like to know the same thing. I said, "Snakes always have a way of slithering in at just the most convenient times."

And it made me think of the garden. Not our Snopes garden, but *the* garden—in Eden.

The first lies uttered on this planet. Making a mess of things for eons. It brought us to this, I knew. Slaying one another for misdeeds and going to bed angry. Mose was right in forgiving people. I wanted to want peace like he did. *God, why wasn't I made more like that?* But, I knew the answer. I had more of Samson in me.

I loved to pursue justice at all costs. The Colt felt natural in my palm. Its heft adjusted to me almost as much as I did it.

The chill of the November air flitted into the saloon and danced across the back of my nape, and I shook. Pickle put a bottle of beer against his neck and shook likewise.

"Mr. Johnson says git, and we stay," Pickle joked.

I paid him little mind. My ears were locked on the sounds of war—night merging with first light. My eyes burned, but I had adrenaline on my side. I needed to see this thing through, or, meet my Maker trying.

Pickle fared less well, as he drooled on the wooden bar, and Mr. Johnson said we both had to get out for real this time. He needed to clean up the drool and check and see if the judge was still alive. I guessed Judge Bigelow was hiding in the harlot's room for as long as possible.

Mr. Johnson shooed us to the swinging doors, and Pickle groggily asked if the war was over.

I heard someone shout, "They're holed up in the courthouse and at Eversole's old fort! I seen 'em make camp!"

Another voice said, "Let's move then. Stop jabbering, you idiot!"

The chaos brought Pickle to life, and I was thankful. He stood on his own two legs, and we broke from the saloon and headed back to the courthouse. I wondered if Judge Bigelow was really still hidden in the saloon.

The shots commenced again, and I ducked behind a barrel—grabbing Pickle, making him do likewise.

The courthouse erupted with return fire and blasts from outside hit the sides of the courthouse with *whack whack* sounds. The Eversoles were dug in deep, and the French party found cover wherever they could on Graveyard Hill. I saw a couple of them sprinting up the hill above the courthouse, and I heard shots from above.

"Who's carryin' on that way?" Pickle asked.

Before I could tell him, I saw a couple of Eversoles rolling down the hill. One sprang up yelling, "Let's get back to the cabin. See if we can git some reinforcements."

The other man stood, too, but limped as he gained his balance—taking off after his partner.

"Hey. If those bastards, Fields and Bad Tom, are up top, we can just stay in the cabin and wait 'em out. Can't we?"

The one in front yelled over his shoulder, "If you wanna be burned alive in that cabin, when they set it afire, you can."

The other passed within feet of me and made sad eye contact.

Pickle started to say something, but I told him to hold off.

The wheels in my brain spun. Then, I looked at Pickle and did an odd thing and smiled. He kept his mouth open and I shushed him.

"Bad Tom, is it?" I said, no longer sounding like myself. More like a ghost or something. It spooked me. Sissy would've told me to not make light of such a serious fix.

Pickle nodded.

"Few things worse than Fult French, huh? I hear tell Bad Tom is the devil himself," I went on.

Pickle didn't argue. He kept quiet as a church mouse.

I lifted both pistols out of their safekeeping and pointed them up the hillside in the direction of the clearing smoke trails. In the direction of Bad Tom. "I want this to end," I said, point blank.

The town was vacant save for some men slowly returning from Eversole's cabin to try and attack Fields and Bad Tom again.

I thought of something and knew it was a decision already made. I nudged Pickle and said I was going with them this time. To fan both pistols and sink some lead into the top of Graveyard Hill. He said he would, too. The more the merrier.

It was the only mission Hazard had provided me. I didn't have Sissy anymore, and Mose wanted to preach one day. *I needed to fight for that, if I didn't do nothing else with my days on earth.* So, I tucked in my pieces and marched head first along with them Eversole boys.

Fields and Bad Tom didn't make it easy. What with their firing at both the courthouse and Eversole's cabin. The firing didn't quit and neither did the return fire. I fell and scratched my knee a time or two and ratcheted by grip on both guns to make sure they were both secure.

As we neared the top of the hill, I felt a sense of déjà vu wash over me. I thought of me and Mose fighting a year ago together. Trying to keep our heads above ground on Shady Mountain. This was different but the same. I was on the offensive now. I wasn't hiding from some unspeakable devil. I was after him. Bad Tom Smith was going to have to show me how bad he really was.

I unlatched the Colt and Remington, cocked the hammers back, *click click.* Pickle did the same with his cheap piece. We marched on alongside some others who didn't question our motives just like we didn't theirs. We wanted the same thing.

A voice called out, "We know you're on foot, and we'll shoot the lot of ye if ye don't quit this foolishness."

We didn't quit and they started firing. Me and Pickle ducked behind two frozen maple trees.

Bullets knocked off tree bark and a few landed in the flesh of fellow warriors. I heard a *grr* and an *argh* sound nearby. Even the fellar who called out, maybe Fields, made a grunting sound.

The firefight continued for at least an hour.

No matter how many times I tried to step out and shoot at Bad Tom someone else got in the way. Apparently these boys wanted him dead just as much as me.

Maybe he shot someone they knew? Or, it could be that he just rubbed them the wrong way. I needed justice in the worst kind of way. The severe kind Judge Bigelow, or Phil, wouldn't dole out. No matter how much I wanted it. So I shot around these Eversole men as best I could. I hit trees and debris all around where Fields and Smith were dug in to what looked like unfilled graves. Bad Tom would spring up and balancing his rifle on a tombstone shoot at us with a mad look about him.

I thought about running right up on them, when Pickle told me one of them was hollering like he was in pain. He said we should wait them out.

Wait them out! Hah! I thought. *I want to see cold bodies no longer breathing.* But, he didn't seem to agree. He wouldn't budge.

Then, before I knew what was happening, Pickle turned and ran down the hillside toward the courthouse. Just like that. *Friends are a dime a dozen,* I figured. Surprisingly, the rest of the Eversole supporters sprinted after him. I checked the numbers and it was just me now. *Why the courthouse? Didn't they know that was even worse? Bad Tom could shoot them from above. God, help me get back to Mose*, I prayed.

Then, I stepped out from behind the maple and shot both guns as many times as I could at the spot where I knew Fields and Smith were lodged inside those empty graves. Again, one of them hollered out in what sounded like pain, and I ran the opposite direction down the hill. To the very courthouse I'd just criticized.

I heard the gunshots behind me, but I didn't feel anything rip into my skin. I made it to the steps and barged through the door. Pickle and the other Eversole fighters nodded at me. One of their crew lay stretched out in the floor. Pickle told me it was Jake McKnight. Two dead now. Campbell and this lad at our feet. He didn't look much older than me. A small red dot on his shirt where his heart rested forever beneath.

I imagined he didn't feel a thing with a single shot like that. I told Pickle I lit into them with everything in both chambers on the way down. He said he heard. It sounded like I was dueling with Satan. *That's what it felt like,* I thought. I asked the lot of them what was next. No one seemed to know, and I said fine, I'd lead.

Shots emptied into the side of the courthouse, and I knew I hadn't killed them all. Some were still up there. Who I couldn't be sure, but I prayed it wasn't Bad Tom, or, the coward, Fult French. The bullets penetrated the sides of the courthouse again, and Judge Bigelow cried out, cowering in the corner.

He wasn't hiding in the harlot's room anymore!

"We got to get out of here or we're gonna look like these church walls," I said nearing the door.

Pickle said he was with me. The others filed into line. I looked them each in the eye and told them to load up with whatever ammunition they had left. This was an all out sprint. Better to go down guns blazing than silent like spooked ghosts. They agreed, not knowing who I was, or why I was so pissed, and pistols were filled full again.

I counted off to three, and we lit out the door in all weather vane directions. Some of the Eversole boys tore off toward the creek and up the opposite hillside. Judge Bigelow even sprang out the door and made for his horse, back to Wolfe County, I guessed. Pickle chased after him, shouting, "Uncle!"

I sprinted head down to where Macho was still tied to the saloon post. Amazingly he was whole and unfilled with bullets. He shook his head in consternation, and I said, "I know. I know, boy. We're all crazy here."

We giddyuped across Canebreak Creek toward home. I didn't have the first clue whether Bad Tom or French was dead or not.

I guessed it didn't matter much in the grand scheme of things. Mose was at the cabin, and Sissy was still dead. Fult French had bought most of the town for a few pieces of silver.

I thanked the good Lord for not letting me get shot. I needed to make peace with my lot in life. According to Mose, I had a lot to live for. We all did. Some purpose. Besides, it wasn't doing me any good shooting these guns. Not one bit.

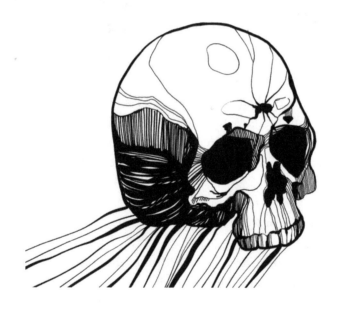

THE END

AUTHOR'S NOTE

A mar on Eastern Kentucky and a story largely untold to those outside Appalachian circles—the French-Eversole feud. Central to this topic was *The Battle of Hazard*. On October 1889, a group of Eversole and French feudists fought in what would lead to several deaths. This feud saw state militia sent directly from Frankfort, the state capital, under the leadership of Sam Hill. It led to Hazard being almost completely abandoned. The retelling of this battle was detailed as sources indicated, despite several listing different names and dates in error. *The Battle of Hazard* included in this illustrated novella was constructed with the assistance of the newspapers below:

November 14, 1889 Salina Daily Republican, Salina, Kansas, Page 1
November 15, 1889 Lawrence Daily Journal, Lawrence, Kansas, Page 1
November 15, 1889 Times Picayune, New Orleans, Louisiana, Page 2
November 15, 1889 The Cincinnati Enquirer, Cincinnati, Ohio, Page 1
November 15, 1889 Detroit Free Press, Detroit, Michigan, Page 2
November 15, 1889 Arkansas City Daily Traveler, Arkansas City, Kansas, Page 8
November 15, 1889 Pittsburgh Daily Post, Pittsburgh, PA, Page 6
November 16, 1889 Scranton Republican, Scranton, PA, Page 1
November 16, 1889 The Times, Philadelphia, PA, Page 4
November 23, 1889 Ohio Democrat, Logan, Ohio, Page 2
December 21, 1889 People's Press, Winston-Salem, NC, Page 3

(The prewar entanglements are purely fictional and should be considered as such.)

The status of two churches at the time in Hazard, KY was fiction. The additional liberty taken was that the first (and only) Catholic Church, Our Mother of Good Counsel Church, in the region didn't arrive until 1913. The church where Preacher Dooley "preached" was entirely made up. In addition to the numerous articles cited, three books were most helpful. First, was the 2009 work *Days of Darkness: The Feuds of Eastern Kentucky*, by Kentucky journalist John Ed Pearce. In it he details several of the most notorious wars amongst families in the region, including the well-known Hatfields & McCoys entanglement. Second, was the 2000 Images of America work, *Hazard, Perry County*, by Martha Hall Quigley. The pictures surrounding the late 1800s, including images of B. Fulton French's quarters. Third, was *History of Perry County, Kentucky* from the Hazard Chapter Daughters of the American Revolution, where many wonderful accounts were given from those traversing the region at the time. These three works helped the battle come to life and give Z Snopes his place.

MY OWN HERITAGE

I hail from the region due west of Leslie & Perry counties. While our region is heavy on emphasizing tourism and Lake Cumberland, the eastern counties (those beyond the I-75 corridor) have relied heavily on coal and its mining. Various jobs afforded me opportunities to meet many wonderful families in the Hazard vicinity. I loved my time there. However, the ill-gotten gains of a few is no new tale. As I watched mountaintop removal take tremendous chunks out of beautiful mountains on the eastern Kentucky/ Pound, Virginia border, I couldn't help but think about the regions gritty past. I, like so many, watched the Hatfields & McCoys series and wondered how many other warring clans existed in this post-Civil War realm. Then, there was the Leonard Elmore *Justified* debut representing a rather biased view of Harlan County, Kentucky where the Wild West appeared as alive as ever in modern day Appalachia. I wanted to know more about the feuds and the spats of those trying to scrape by, while the nation was said to be 'reconstructing.' It led me to the greed of a single man, Benjamin Fulton French, and his need to do more than just survive in Kentucky. His need to swindle landowners out of their homes, for a little bit of coal, intrigued me and broke my heart. I researched accounts of his conflicts with Joseph Eversole, and I kept thinking about how a poor family would manage at such a time. I wanted to try and recreate this time in an illustrated format, and I hope this novella does create some semblance of how it actually was.

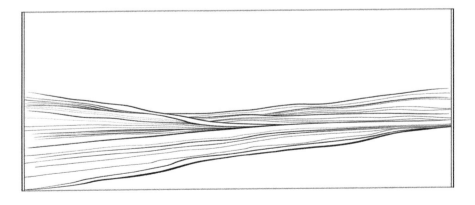

ACKNOWLEDGMENTS

To my wife, who knows how to make this world better. Proof of God is present every morning I see you, L.

To Mom and Dad, who saw me grow and mature into someone I pray they are proud of.

To Jared, my brother, who is the reason I left baseball and played 'real' sports. His adventurous spirit molded my sisters and me into what we are. May we never go knee-boarding again.

To Nathan Davis, who is a friend I cherish for having written and composed countless rebuttals to ideas and wacky plans I'm concocted over the years.

To the UTC Team, who provides the best work environment imaginable in the hallowed halls of college.

To Reagan Rothe and *Black Rose Writing* for taking a chance with me and this labor of love.

To Christopher Dixson and Jesse Graves, who embraced *Swimming the Echo* and allowed this newest work to receive the attention it needed.

To Bluegrass Writers Studio and EKU MFA alum, who supported and encouraged me from miles away.

To Russell Helms, who always welcomed a Chattanooga Billiards run, and for writing fiction that inspires. If you haven't read his work, DO IT!

To Star Line Books and its wonderful staff for accepting Chattanooga writers over the years—thank you for making 'story time' fun again.

To Dani Pinto Pyles, who slammed me into a locker in sixth grade and told me to stay out of her way.

To BookIt, for making me want to read.

To Wendell Berry, who told me work wasn't a four-letter word.

To The Meeting House, who supplied coffee and cookies every Saturday morning.

To Thomas Merton for choosing Gethsemani and contemplating life.

To MHS, for unlocking mysteries, and providing a creative outlet each and every day (Saucy Sledge, too) from grade school to graduation. You will be forever missed, forever cherished on Cave Street!

DISCUSSION QUESTIONS

1. *Pokeweed* is set in post-Civil War America. How does the violence described impact those involved in Hazard, Kentucky? Does it bring to mind any other episodes in American history?

2. With all of the recent school shootings, think about how this town's education suffers in the midst of the violence? How does it impact Z's community, his neighbors?

3. How do the illustrations complement the subject of this book: *The French-Eversole Feud*?

4. If you were making *Pokeweed* into a movie, who would be in it? Why?

5. What's your favorite quote? Why does that particular quote stand out?

6. What emotions does this novella stir in you?

7. What songs does this book make you think of?

8. If you could ask the author one question, what would it be?

9. If you could meet one character in real life, who would you choose?

10. What do you think of the book's cover? How well does it describe the story?

11. What do you think the author's purpose was in writing this book? What ideas was he trying to convey?

12. How original and unique was this book to you?

13. If you could hear this same story from another person's point of view, who would you choose?

14. How well do you think the author built the world in the book?

15. Did the characters seem believable to you? Did they remind you of anyone you know?

View other Black Rose Writing titles at www.blackrosewriting.com/books

and use promo code **PRINT** to receive a **20% discount** when purchasing.

BLACK ROSE
writing™

CPSIA information can be obtained
at www.ICGtesting.com
Printed in the USA
LVHW11s0550190918
590475LV00001B/53/P